Andrew Br

Puffin Books
Editor: Kaye Webb

THUNDER AND LIGHTNINGS

As well as being an interesting story, this is a book
about a friendship. And a rather unexpected one at that.
For what interests could bright Andrew, whose family
had just moved to Tiler's Cottage – father working
with computers, mother an ex-librarian – have in common
with the local boy whom teachers thought backward?
The answer was Lightnings – the beautiful, doomed
aeroplanes that filled the wide Norfolk
sky with their roaring magnificence every time they
flew from R.A.F. Coltishall.

Victor knew more about aeroplanes than anyone
Andrew had ever met. His room was full of models
and pictures. His lamp was specially dimmed so that it
looked like a bomber's moon. Andrew was fascinated by
Victor's devotion to planes, but as the friendship grew,
Andrew became more and more worried about what
would happen to Victor when he discovered that his
beloved Lightnings were to be replaced by Jaguars . . .

Thunder and Lightnings, winner of the Penguin/Guardian
competition, and the Carnegie Medal for 1976, is Jan
Mark's first book. Her second, *Under the Autumn Garden*,
is also in Puffins. For readers of nine and over.

JAN MARK

Thunder and Lightnings

Illustrated by Jim Russell

PUFFIN BOOKS

Puffin Books, Penguin Books Ltd, Harmondsworth,
Middlesex, England
Penguin Books, 625 Madison Avenue,
New York, New York 10022, U.S.A.
Penguin Books Australia Ltd, Ringwood,
Victoria, Australia
Penguin Books Canada Ltd, 2801 John Street,
Markham, Ontario, Canada L3R 1B4
Penguin Books (N.Z.) Ltd, 182–190 Wairau Road,
Auckland 10, New Zealand

First published by Kestrel Books 1976
Published in Puffin Books 1978
Reprinted 1979, 1980

Text copyright © Jan Mark, 1976
Illustrations copyright © Jim Russell, 1976
All rights reserved

Made and printed in Great Britain by
Richard Clay (The Chaucer Press) Ltd,
Bungay, Suffolk

For David and Faith

Contents

1 | Low Flying

When the car stopped Andrew was the first to get out.

Since they left the old house, four hours ago, he had been trapped in the back, wedged between the carry-cot and the guinea-pig hutch. On one side Edward growled to himself in the carry-cot and on the other the guinea-pigs whistled fretfully.

Andrew climbed over the hutch and was out on the road before Mum had switched off the engine. He had been sitting in one position for so long that his knees cracked when he tried to straighten them. On the far side of the car, Dad climbed out with all the maps on his lap. Andrew heard them slither to the ground, one after the other.

Mum was the last out. She was also the tallest, which was why she was driving, with the seat pushed back as far as it would go, instead of navigating in the passenger seat, which was pushed forward to make room for the crate of beer bottles behind it.

' "Only three hours to Pallingham," ' said Mum, quoting something that Dad had said earlier, before they set out. 'Eighty minutes to the hour, by my watch.'

'You should have followed my directions, I had the maps,' said Dad, scrabbling for them underneath the car.

'If I'd followed your directions we'd be a mile out to sea by now, and heading for Denmark.'

Andrew left them arguing and crossed the lane to look at the new house. All he could see from the car was a gate in the hedge and the name on it. 'Tiler's Cottage'. He had hoped that a country cottage would be thatched but presumably a tiler wouldn't have thatch on his roof.

He could see very little more from across the lane. The house was long and low, lurking behind the bushes with its head down. The only visible part was the roof, tiled, with a window in it. He had been promised the attic room for his own, but he noticed that the window was broken. He wondered what kind of a view he would get through it and turned round to look.

It was all sky.

Apart from the house and the hedge it was all sky. He had always imagined that if you lived in a flat place you could see for miles across the rolling plains but now he found that it wasn't so. The horizon was in the next field.

It was a field of furry barley. Andrew, having lived all his life in towns, had never seen barley except in a photograph. He was rather pleased to see it alive and growing in a Norfolk field. The geography master had taught Andrew that Norfolk was flat, fertile, and full of water. Andrew had never found any good reason for believing what he was told in geography lessons, so he was almost surprised to find that it wasn't a mountainous desert, littered with bones.

The field opposite the house was full of green plants that looked like beetroot disguised as cabbage.

'Sugar beet,' said Dad, coming up behind him. 'You'll see it growing all over East Anglia. Come and give us a hand with the livestock, will you?'

Andrew went back to the car and picked up the guinea-pig hutch which was resting on the bonnet. Mum was carrying Edward; Dad had the crate of beer bottles. He made his own beer and the bottles were all dead men, waiting for the next brew.

They went into the garden and Mum pulled up the house agent's sign with SOLD stuck on it and put it down behind the hedge.

'All ours, now,' she said. Dad unlocked the front door and they went in.

There was no hall. The door led straight into the living room, dark and haunted by the smell of the last owner's last meal. To the right was a little slip room where the stairs went up. Ahead, another door led into the kitchen. The doorway was so low that Dad's hair brushed the lintel as he went through. Mum followed and hit her head on it.

Andrew wanted to explore, but he was sent back to the gate to flag down the removal van as it came down the lane.

'Otherwise it will go straight past and all our furniture will be carried on to Yarmouth and points East,' said Dad.

'East of Yarmouth is the sea,' said Mum. 'I wish you'd take my headroom into account, next time you chance to be buying a house.'

Andrew went out and took up position on the bank opposite the front gate. There was a long drop into the sugar beet. Looking down, he noticed a rat prancing through the beets. He had always understood rats to be poisonous and dangerous but this rat was clean and genial-looking: a country rat. He stood upright to look around him. Being a little higher meant that he could see further but not very much. Beyond the beet was a tall hedge, then the sky again.

He stood astride the bank and stared up into it, until his eyes went out of focus and his head became so hollow that when he looked down he could see sky underneath him as well as above.

There seemed to be no sound at all.

Then he heard a far-off growl, as faint as a lorry crossing a distant bridge. He scanned the sky until he discovered where it was coming from. Immediately overhead a tiny, dark dot was moving, so slowly that at first he could not be sure that it moved at all. At once, the little sound changed to a furious roar, so suddenly that he half expected to see the sky crazed all over like a cracked bowl. Across the fields came a vicious black aircraft, so low he thought he could have touched it, only when it passed over him he was crouched on the bank with his head down. When he looked up after it, it was no more than a thin slit in the sky out of which rolled wave after wave of booming sound.

'Are we being dive-bombed?' asked Mum, over the gate.

'It was a jet,' said Andrew. 'I never saw it coming. I thought it was going to crash but it went up again. I didn't even hear it till it got here. I was watching another one, higher up.'

He looked, and saw the dot, still cruising above him, unheard now in the backwash of the jet engines, already below the horizon.

'I wonder if that happens very often,' said Mum. Andrew's ears ached. He thought he heard the aircraft coming back again, but it was only the removal van, all forgotten, turning the corner at the end of the lane.

When all the furniture was in and the removal men had drunk their tea and gone away, Mum put Edward in his cot and they sat down to tea in the kitchen. It was a much disturbed meal, for every time they heard an aircraft coming, they rushed outside to see what it was: but the planes flew so fast and so low that there was never time to identify them except in the case of the helicopter that dawdled over, last of all. It was sleek and striped, like a long-distance coach with a rotor on the roof.

'It's as good as Farnborough,' said Dad, 'without the bother of having to go there.'

'Did you know about the aeroplanes when you bought the house?' asked Mum. 'Were you saving them up as a lovely surprise for me?'

'Cross my heart,' said Dad. 'They weren't flying when I was last up here. All I saw was the helicopter.'

Andrew wasn't sure whose side he was on. Although he quite liked watching aeroplanes he had only seen them at close quarters from the observation platform at Gatwick Airport, rather like seeing savage animals safely behind bars at the zoo. Having them at large, all over the sky was a different matter entirely.

Mum put Edward to bed behind battlements of cardboard boxes and Andrew climbed to his attic with a piece of polythene and adhesive tape to mend his window.

'We'll get a piece of glass for that soon,' said Mum, calling upstairs from the landing. Andrew thought that probably it would not be soon.

The attic room was small and not very light, but it

was exactly the kind of room that he wanted. He stood in the middle of it deciding where he would have his wardrobe, his bookcase and his bed which was at present standing on end, behind the door. By the window, the roof sloped right down to the floor. If he put the bed there it would be just like sleeping in a tent.

There was a ledge built into the wall beside it, where he could set up his race track. He opened the tea-chest that contained his belongings and lifting out the ludo board that held them down, began to unpack his racing cars. They were all Formula One, carefully painted in real team colours. He lined them up where the grid was going to be, except for the one that had lost a wheel and was permanently in the pits. There was also one that had been run over by a full-sized car – his father's – and was useless, except for staging shunts.

He selected his favourite and placed it in pole position and knelt beside the shelf, gently pushing the car back and forth with his finger and thinking that whole squadrons of supersonic fighters could not make up for living a hundred and fifty miles from Brand's Hatch. When Dad had said that they were going to live in the country, no one but Andrew had taken that into consideration.

'There's plenty of country in Kent,' he said.

'Plenty of expensive country,' said Dad, so now they were going to live in Norfolk, surrounded by mad fighter pilots and miles from the nearest race track, unless you counted Snetterton. Andrew didn't. Not after Brand's Hatch.

A chilly wind, blowing through the broken window

pane, reminded him that he had come up there to mend it. He left the cars and went over to the window to look out. Now that he could see it properly the view was much larger. Beyond the hedge at the end of the beet field was a row of sheds and a toppling straw stack. By leaning out of the window he could see two church towers, a windmill and yet another tower painted in red and white stripes. He wondered if it could be a lighthouse and guessed that the flat place where earth met sky was the coast.

He stuck his piece of polythene over the broken pane and went downstairs. From the landing window the view had shrunk again, but he noticed a roof showing above the trees, further down the road. It must belong to their next door neighbours, three fields away.

As he was looking out he heard a tremendous thud at the back of his head and a thousand miles away at the same time. He left the window swinging and ran down to the ground floor. Dad was at the foot of the stairs.

'What was that, was it a bomb?' said Andrew.

'No, it wasn't. Bombs don't sound like that at all,' said Dad. He went into the living room and opened the front door. 'Listen.'

Far off and very high, they heard a jet engine.

'Sonic boom,' said Dad. 'Surely you've heard one before?'

'Not like that,' said Andrew. 'Was that plane breaking the sound barrier, then?'

Without thinking about it very much, he imagined the sound barrier as a high, corrugated iron fence in the sky, falling down in sections where aircraft went through it. He knew perfectly well that it was not, but he could even see it, dull red and full of rusty holes. He had first thought of it like that when he was very small and he suspected that even if he ever broke the sound barrier himself, he would never quite get rid of that fence.

2 | Open Country

Mum and Andrew met on the landing early in the morning.

'Creep past Edward's door,' said Mum. 'I don't want him to wake up yet. I fancy a cup of tea in peace, first.'

In the kitchen the guinea-pigs whistled in their hutch under the sink. Someone had left the window open all night and there were dirty paw-prints up and down the floor, in front of the hutch. On the draining board lay something that looked like an old dishcloth. The dishcloth unfolded itself and stood up. It was a big, thin ginger cat with muddy feet.

'Hullo, Ginger,' said Mum. 'You needn't think you're staying, because you're not.' She gave him some milk and put him out. He disappeared into the hedge but after breakfast he was back again, lying on the wire roof of the hutch. The guinea-pigs sat in their straw, staring up at him. Andrew tried to imagine their view of him, pressed into a hairy quilt by the chicken wire. Once again Mum gave him milk and put him out of the door. He sat on the window sill and beamed at them. He knew that they would let him in eventually.

By lunch time he was asleep on the settee in the living room.

Lunch was an untidy meal, eaten all over the house and involving a great deal of bread and a very little cheese.

'This won't do,' said Mum. 'We must have food. Someone will have to go into town.'

'Polthorpe's about two miles away,' said Dad. 'But I noticed a sort of shop by the church when we passed it yesterday.'

'Who wants a walk then?' said Mum. 'Andrew does.'

'No, I don't,' said Andrew.

'Yes, you do,' said Mum.'Get the map and see if you can find your way round.'

Andrew searched among the maps for one that gave a close-up view of Pallingham village.

'It must be here somewhere,' said Dad, 'I bought it especially.'

'It's probably still under the car,' said Mum. Andrew went out to look and found the map lying damply in the road where Dad had dropped it the day before. He laid it out on the living room floor and Ginger stepped down from the settee and sat in the middle of it like a castaway on a raft. Andrew moved his tail which was lying along the coast and concealing a strip of country, two miles wide. Tiler's Cottage actually appeared on the map as a small black dot. Andrew felt quite famous, living in a house that was shown on a map.

A little way past the house a footpath was marked in red. It snaked across blank, white fields and ended in the churchyard. Andrew decided to try to follow it. The journey by road seemed rather too long to attempt on his first trip.

Ten minutes later he found himself alone in the fields with a shopping basket and the map. When he set out, the house had been on his left and the church straight ahead. Now, the house and the church were on his right. Somewhere he had left the path and strayed onto the headland of the barley field which, seen close to, was not furry at all, but full of spikey whiskers.

He put down the shopping bag and spread out the map on the ground. Now that he no longer knew where he was the map was no help and he saw that he had put it down next to a very dead mouse. He folded it up again and retraced his steps until he reached the place where he should have turned aside. He squeezed between the hedge and a clump of fierce nettles, and there was nothing between him and the churchyard but a field of pale wheat. Wheat was yellow in pictures: this was the colour of sand. It reached his chest and he trailed his arm through it, watching it ripple back into place as though he had never been there. It rustled dryly behind him.

He was halfway across before he saw the aircraft heading towards him, over the wheat. Experienced, after yesterday, he had his arms wrapped round his head before the sound reached him, only a second or two before the aircraft did. First he was blotted out by its shadow, then by the blistering roar of its jets. He hardly saw what it looked like, a black bat that whipped round the church tower so closely that he was sure that it would hit it. When he looked up again, though, the tower was still there and the aircraft had vanished, leaving only an angry rumble behind it. Andrew gathered speed across the wheat field and ran through the iron gateway, into the churchyard. An old man was kneeling by one of the graves, cutting grass. When the second fighter went over, Andrew ducked against a headstone but the old man went on snipping: as though nothing larger than a butterfly had passed.

'Do they always fly so low?' asked Andrew. The old man shrugged.

'Sometimes they do,' he said, 'and sometimes they don't.'

'What was it?' said Andrew.

'An aeroplane,' said the old man, going clip, clip, clip, very carefully, round the bottom of the gravestone. 'I reckon they use that old tower as a marker, to see their way home. I shot one down, once.'

'One of them?' said Andrew, pointing to the gap in the sky where the jets had gone.

'No. During the war. Ack–Ack,' said the old man. 'They was slower, then.' He laughed, but Andrew could see that he wasn't interested in aeroplanes any more. He was too close to the ground.

Andrew went on, round the corner of the church. There wasn't a house in sight except for the two opposite the churchyard gate, and one of those was a pub. The other was the shop, so he crossed the road and went in.

The shop was divided into two. One end was a Post Office and the other was fitted out like a supermarket with long shelves and wire baskets although it was no bigger than the kitchen at home. He went round with a basket collecting tins and packets, including meat for Ginger although it wasn't on his list. Mum said Ginger must be on his way by bedtime but Andrew, and Ginger, knew better.

At the back of the shop and almost hidden in the shadow behind the Post Office grille, a small old lady was watching television on a portable set that stood on a cardboard box at the end of the counter.

'That's the schools' broadcast,' she said, when he came round to pay. 'I always watch the schools. Why aren't you at school?'

'We've only just moved in. We came yesterday,' said Andrew. 'I'll go to school next term.'

'I never went to school at all,' said the old lady, unpacking the basket. 'I was too ill. I was ill all the time I should have been at school. I got better though, soon as that was time to leave. The day I should have left, I got better in no time. I can add up, though. Two pounds, five shillings and sixpence. I don't need a cash register.'

Andrew had been working out the total as he went round in case he didn't have enough money. 'Two pounds, twenty-seven and a half pence,' he said.

'Two pounds, five and six,' said the old lady. 'In money. Do you like school?'

'Not much,' said Andrew.

'You'd better get ill, then,' said the old lady. 'I had a weak chest. Nobody could prove different.'

'I think they could nowadays,' said Andrew. 'They'd cure it, too.'

'Too clever to live, doctors,' said the old lady. Andrew returned home, envious for the days when you could invent an illness for years at a time and never get caught.

When he got back he told Mum about the old lady in the shop and how she had managed to avoid going to school. As soon as he had finished he saw that he would have been wiser to say nothing. Talking about school had given Mum ideas.

'If you're going to school this term I'd better drop by and see the headmaster,' she said. 'He'll probably let you start at once.'

'I don't want to start at once,' said Andrew. 'It's only about two weeks to the end of term. Can't I just have a long holiday?'

'He'll wonder if you don't turn up,' said Mum. 'Because Dad wrote and told him you'd be coming. I'll see to it tomorrow.'

Andrew lifted Ginger onto his lap and tried to play with him but he had a nasty, sucked-away feeling inside, all the way down from his ribs to his knees. He wished that he could go pale and sweaty when he felt ill, so that people would know just how ill he was. He put the cat down and managed, at the same time, to take a look at himself in the bathroom mirror which was propped against the dresser, waiting to be hung. He looked as healthy as he had feared, especially with his face pink from being upside down. If he suddenly developed a weak chest he would be rumbled at once.

'If you start now,' said Mum, 'you might make a friend or two and then you'll know your way about, next term. Anyway, I don't think that this school will be quite the same as your last one.'

'Certainly not,' said Dad. 'I drove past it when I came to look over the house and I distinctly saw people in the playground, walking upright.'

'Everybody walks upright,' said Andrew.

'Not at the Gasworks,' said Dad. 'Their knuckles scraped the ground. The evening air was rent by the cries of the First Eleven, swinging through the girders on their way to the playing field. The Second Eleven went on all fours.'

'It was the Glasswell, not the Gasworks,' said Andrew. 'It was named after the mayor, or somebody dead, or something.'

'Glasswell, Gasworks, let's face it, you didn't think much of it,' said Mum. 'Better luck this time. I'll go in tomorrow and arrange it.'

Next morning they all had something to do. Mum went off to the school in Polthorpe, Dad set about wiring up the hi-fi system and Edward settled down in his playpen to finish pulling the stuffing out of his woolly elephant.

Andrew went into the garden to assemble his patent, monococque, guinea-pig pen. It was his own invention; a tube of chicken wire, three feet across, with a circular piece of wire at each end. To erect it he had to cut away a rectangle of grass from the lawn, lay the wire lengthways on the bare earth and then put the turf back inside the pen so that the floor of it was grass and the guinea-pigs could not burrow their way out.

He was rather proud of his invention. It was the only thing that he had ever invented and he wondered if there was a special magazine for guinea-pig enthusiasts to which he could send the plans. People all over the country might be glad to know how to make one, but he was afraid that if he did it might turn out not to be his own idea after all and that people all over the country would have built their own already.

The chicken wire had been badly dented in transit. The removal men had not noticed that it was meant to be a patent, monococque, guinea-pig pen and had stood the lawnmower on it. It took him a long time to straighten out the wire into a neat cylinder. When he had finished planting it he stood back to admire his work and observed that he had set it up directly under the washing line. When Mum hung out the washing she would have to climb over it. Not that she was likely to complain; it was the kind of thing she would do herself, but he knew that if he had been attending to the job he would have sited it better. All the time he had been wondering how Mum was getting on at the school.

He went indoors to fetch the guinea-pigs and found that the loudspeaker cabinets had worked their way out of the living room and into the kitchen, trailing flex and crocodile clips. Dad was busy with a screwdriver in the doorway.

'You weren't thinking of making us a drink, were you?' said Dad, without moving his lips. He was holding three strands of wire between his teeth.

'If I switch on will you light up?' said Andrew.

'Try it and see,' said Dad. 'Just try it. You'll have to make tea again, the percolator's still packed.'

'Good,' muttered Andrew, thinking of the murky liquid that came out of the percolator. He went to put the kettle on but the soldering iron was plugged into the socket and little drops of solder lay all over the draining board. They looked like blobs of spilled mercury and reminded Andrew of an incident at his last school. Everyone in the class had borrowed a bit of mercury to play with while the chemistry teacher was out of the room, but it was Andrew who had upset the bottle.

'I'll make the tea when you've finished,' he said and took the guinea-pigs' hutch outside. They were tired

25

of being moved about and hung from his hands like old fur gloves when he lifted them into the pen. They felt uneasy on alien grass and sat sulking in the corner. He connected the hutch to the pen with a little tunnel of wire netting and put in fresh food and water, but they ignored him and grumbled together with their backs turned. He thought he knew how they felt.

He sat down on the grass with his back against the hutch and picked the mud from under his fingernails with the wirecutters. It was very quiet. Apart from the helicopter churning across the sky there was nothing flying today. In the stillness he became aware of a series of explosions in the distance. Every now and then there would be a loud bang followed by rolling echoes. While he was working the wind had changed and the latest bang sounded so close that he jumped and then got up, pretending that the jump had been part of the getting-up process in case anyone was watching through the hedge. He went indoors.

'Dad, do you think there's a rifle range round here?' Then he stopped. Mum had come home. She was making the tea herself.

'It looks a nice enough school,' she said, when she saw Andrew hesitating in the doorway. 'Nobody threw anything and one chap held a door open for me. You can start on Monday. You'll be in class 1a for the rest of this term.'

Andrew felt a sad pain coming behind his eyes and went outside again. Monday was only five days away.

3 | First Day, Worst Day

Dad offered to drive him to school on Monday morning.

At first he thought it was a good idea as it would give him less time to think about where he was going while he got there, but by Sunday evening he had changed his mind. Walking to the bus stop, getting on the bus, buying a ticket and getting off again would lessen the shock when he arrived; like lowering himself very slowly into a cold bath. He saw himself doing all these things and then he saw himself losing his fare, missing the bus, or getting off at the wrong stop, and he began to feel weak again.

They were all sitting round the kitchen table after tea. Dad was filleting a transistor radio among the breadcrumbs and whistling through his teeth. He could afford to whistle. He was still on holiday.

Mum was picking the badge off his blazer to replace it with the one she had bought in Polthorpe. The new one was red with a gold stripe across it. The old one had a lion and three bottles on it; at least they looked like bottles and he had never discovered what they were meant to be. It didn't matter any more, he would never go back.

Dad was laying out transistors round the edge of his plate like someone playing at Cherrystones. Andrew's plate was already heaped with pieces of wire and solder. It looked like a meal for robots.

'Don't brood,' said Mum as she saw him staring at his plate. 'The first day's always the worst. After that, you know what to expect.'

'You said that when I started my last school,' said Andrew, 'and that got worse and worse.'

He went up to his room and pushed the racing cars about for a bit. Tonight they looked tinny and feeble and he could see, more clearly than usual, the messy bits where his paintbrush had faltered. Then he reached into the almost empty tea-chest and pulled out his satchel. The strap had come off and there was a big stain inside, where someone had poured ink into it. Apart from the stain there was nothing but his pencil case and a piece of paper with a rude message on it. Andrew opened the pencil box and out fell a rubber, decorated with teeth marks. He tried to fit his own teeth into the dents, but they must have been bitten by someone else.

Then he found a lump on his neck and hoped that his tonsils might be swelling up but he couldn't make them hurt, no matter how hard he prodded. He looked at his watch. It was a quarter to nine. He thought, in exactly twelve hours' time the bus will be stopping in Polthorpe and I shall be walking up the path into school. The very thought was enough to give him a clutching sort of pain, exactly where he thought his heart must be, but it passed away, almost before he had time to feel it. He went over to the window and looked out, kneeling on the floor with his chin wedged against the sill. Down below, in the dusk, the gunman sauntered by, his ferocious face half hidden by the up-turned collar of his coat.

Every evening, at half past six, he walked up the

lane with a shotgun tucked under his arm. Sooner or later, they heard his footsteps as he came back again, still scowling at his boots and looking neither right nor left. Andrew feared the sight of him, not because he had a gun, but because he never spoke, never looked up, only passed in dark silence, up and down the lane.

Every time he heard the unexplained explosions rolling across the fields he thought of the gunman and once, when a very loud one woke him in the night, he saw a black vision of the gunman, standing at the gate and waiting, his gun to his shoulder.

He looked at his watch again. It was nine o'clock.

In exactly twelve hours time he would be in school.

Next morning he found that he didn't have to walk up the path into school after all. 1a was housed in a mobile classroom at the end of the playground, next to the cemetery. The quickest way in was through a hole in the fence, behind the cycle sheds. He was given a seat at the back, by the window and when he looked out he could see the gravestones, white and shiny and all the same height, like false teeth: neater than the old tusks in Pallingham churchyard but not so interesting. He answered to his name on the register, paid his lunch money and was handed a timetable to copy, which he thought was a waste of time as it was only current for the next two weeks. After assembly he spent the rest of the day trailing round the school, looking for the right classrooms and wandering into the wrong ones and discovering that the timetable was inaccurate anyway.

No one had any time for him. The boys were busy and fast on their feet. The girls kept very much to themselves, gathering in giggling huddles in the playground and sitting on their own side in class: except for Jeannette Butler who was bold and sat with the boys, knocking them about with a strong right arm if they cheeked her.

However, by the end of the day he had decided that this school was better than the last one even though he didn't like it. Nobody had offered to pull his head off, rip his coat or throw his shoes over the roof. On the other hand, nobody had spoken to him, either.

By Thursday afternoon, nothing had changed. Andrew was not entirely surprised. No one spoke to him because no one knew he was there. Every day he found himself with a different group and he only saw his own class altogether at registration. After that they were split up for almost every lesson. Maths with Ix, English with Ic, Games with IIy, a lesson mysteriously entitled G.S. with Iz. At the end of that period he was no wiser about G.S. than he had been at the beginning. It seemed that the class was working from page 135 in Book Two while the teacher was on page 135 of Book Three. As both books had identical covers the lesson was over before anyone noticed. Andrew had had no book anyway, being advised to share with a boy in a pink shirt who kept his elbow firmly between Andrew and the book. When the bell rang Andrew grabbed the boy in the pink shirt before he could leave.

'What was all that about?'

'I dunno,' said the boy, detaching his pink sleeve from Andrew's grasp and treading on Andrew's feet in order to be out of the room first. 'Don't ask me,' he said. 'We don't usually have books. We don't usually have Bacon-rind either.'

'Bacon-rind?'

'Mr Baker, Bacon-rind. He don't know what he's doing. Nor do we. Miss Beale ought to take us but she's been away. She'll be back tomorrow, Sir said.'

Andrew looked at his timetable and saw that G.S. was scheduled to take up the whole of Friday morning.

'Here, what is G.S.?' he asked, as they jostled down the corridor.

'I dunno. General Subjects or General Studies, or something. We got Private Study on Fridays as well. Last lesson.'

Andrew thought he would make a joke.

'When do we have Sergeant-Major Studies?' he said.

The boy in the pink shirt thought this was so funny, or unfunny, that he gave at the knees, fell against the wall, hit himself on the head and staggered away down the corridor, reeling from side to side and howling with phoney laughter.

Andrew consulted his timetable and saw that it was time to go home. This didn't necessarily mean that it *was* time to go home, but he decided to give it the benefit of the doubt and headed for the cloakroom.

4 | Victor

On Friday morning Andrew arrived early for the
lesson and stationed himself by the teacher's desk,
determined to get some information before he did
anything else. While he was waiting, he looked round
the room to see if there were any survivors from the
last lesson and decided that there were at least three
people that he had seen before: Jeannette Butler,
the boy in the pink shirt and another boy whose ap-
pearance worried Andrew because he was sure there
was something wrong with him. He was hideously
swollen about the body but very thin in the face.
Andrew leaned against the desk and wondered
what kind of disease could possibly cause a person to
become such a horrid shape. The boy's spindly legs
seemed hardly strong enough to support the rest of
him.

'You're the new boy, are you?' said someone beside
him. 'I'm Miss Beale, who are you?'

'I'm Mitchell,' said Andrew. 'Andrew Mitchell,
Miss.' It sounded like a silly sort of tongue twister.

'How do you like it here?' said Miss Beale. Andrew
didn't intend to be side-tracked.

"What are we supposed to be doing?' he asked.

'That rather depends on you,' said Miss Beale. 'In
General Studies you can choose your own subject and
follow it through. You'll be rather behind the others
but you can start on a project now and work on it

through the holidays. That's what most of the others will do, if they haven't finished by next week.'

Andrew found this hard to believe.

'What are you interested in?' asked Miss Beale.

'Motor racing, guinea-pigs,' said Andrew.

'Well, either of those would do for a start,' said Miss Beale. 'Perhaps Victor would show you round so that you can see how the others set about it.' Andrew thought she wanted to be rid of him and when he turned round he found that a restive queue had formed behind him. Miss Beale directed him to Victor. He was the very fat boy with the very thin face.

Andrew was reluctant to go any closer. How could he stroll up and hold a normal conversation with anyone so deformed? He picked up his satchel and walked casually round the fat boy's desk as though he just happened to be passing it. When he got close, Andrew realized that Victor was not fat at all. On the contrary, he was exceptionally thin; all of him, not just his head and legs. The fat part was made up of clothes. Andrew could see a white T-shirt, a red shirt, a blue sweater and a red sweater. Further down he wore a pair of black jeans with orange patches sewn over the knees and yellow patches on the hip pockets. Over it all he had an anorak so covered in badges and buttons that it was difficult to tell what colour it was.

In fact, he was not so much dressed as camouflaged. Even his hair seemed to be some part of a disguise, more like a wig than live hair, dusty black as if it had been kicked round the floor before being put on. It was so long at the front that Victor was actually looking through it. His ears stuck out cheerfully, like a Radar device.

'Miss Beale said you would show me round, to look at the projects,' said Andrew.

'Why, do you want to copy one?' asked Victor, lifting a strand of hair and exposing one eye. 'You could copy mine, only someone might recognize it. I've done that three times already.'

'Whatever for?' said Andrew. 'Don't you get tired of it?'

Victor shook his head and his hair.

'That's only once a year. I did that two times at the junior school and now I'm doing that again,' he said. 'I do fish, every time. Fish are easy. They're all the same shape.'

'No, they're not,' said Andrew.

'They are when I do them,' said Victor. He spun his book round, with one finger, to show Andrew the drawings. His fish were not only all the same shape, they were all the same shape as slugs. Underneath each drawing was a printed heading: BRAEM; TENSH; CARP; STIKLBAK; SHARK. It was the only way of telling them apart. The shark and the bream were identical, except that the shark had a row of teeth like tank traps.

'Isn't there a "c" in stickleback?' said Andrew. Victor looked at his work.

'You're right.' He crossed out both 'k's, substituted 'c's and pushed the book away, the better to study it. 'I got that wrong last year.'

Andrew flipped over a few pages. There were more slugs: PLACE; COD; SAWFISH; and a stringy thing with a frill round its neck: EEL.

'Don't you have to write anything?' asked Andrew.

'Yes, look. I wrote a bit back here. About every four pages will do,' said Victor. 'Miss Beale, she keep saying I ought to write more but she's glad when I don't. She's got to read it. Nobody can read my writing.'

Andrew was not surprised. Victor's writing was a sort of code to deceive the enemy, with punctuation marks in unlikely places to confuse anyone who came too close to cracking the code. He watched Andrew counting the full stops in one sentence and said, 'I put those in while I think about the next word. I like doing question marks better.' He pointed out two or three specimens, independent question marks, without questions. They looked like curled feathers out of a pillow. One had a face.

'Do you put a question mark in every sentence?' said Andrew.

'Oh, yes. I know you don't actually need them,' said Victor, 'but they're nice to do.'

Andrew turned to the last page of the book. There was a drawing of a whale.

'Whales aren't fish,' said Andrew.

'Aren't they?' said Victor. 'Are you sure? I always put a whale in.'

'Whales are mammals.'

'What's a mammal?' said Victor. He wrote 'This.is. not.a.fish?' under his whale and closed the book. 'Come and see the others.'

'Mammals don't lay eggs,' said Andrew, as they set off round the room.

'That's a pity,' said Victor. 'I'd like to see a whale's egg. Big as a bath, wouldn't that be?' He stopped by the boy in the pink shirt. 'Let's have a look at your project, Tim.'

Andrew thought he had seen most of Tim's project

before. It featured a man in a tree, knotty with muscles and wearing a leopard skin.

'Tarzan,' said Tim.

'Why do a project about Tarzan?' said Andrew.

'Tarzan's easy,' said Tim. 'You just cut him out and stick him in.'

'Fish are easier,' said Victor.

'Why not do worms then?' said Andrew. 'Nothing could be easier than worms. Wiggle-wiggle-wiggle: all over in a second. Page one, worms are long and thin. Page two, worms are round.'

Victor began to grin but Tim sat down to give the idea serious consideration.

Victor's grin became wider, revealing teeth like Stonehenge.

'I reckon you're catching on,' he said. 'Why don't you do worms?'

'I want to do something interesting,' said Andrew.

'Ho,' said Victor. 'You'll come to a bad end, you will.'

They went on round the room. Andrew noticed that nearly all the boys were doing a project on fish or fishing. The girls tended to specialize in horses except for Jeannette Butler, who wouldn't let them see hers.

'Why don't you go and stand in the road and catch cars?' said Jeannette, giving them a hefty shove when they tried to look.

'Give us a kiss,' said Victor and got a poke in the chest instead.

'I think I'll do motor racing,' said Andrew when they got back to Victor's desk. 'I know a bit about that, already. Me and my Dad used to go to Brand's Hatch a lot, when we lived in Kent.'

'Where's Kent?' said Victor. 'Down at the bottom somewhere, isn't it?'

'Some of it is,' said Andrew. 'We were further up, near London.' Andrew fetched a piece of drawing paper and sat down to draw a Formula One racing car. Victor drew some scales on his whale and broadcast punctuation marks throughout the book, letting them fall wherever he fancied.

At the end of the lesson the group split up again. Andrew thought he had seen the last of Victor who elbowed his way out of the room and was lost from sight in the roaring mob that boiled towards the canteen. Andrew followed on his own, consumed with disappointment. During the lesson it had seemed as though he might have found a friend. He wondered if he had offended Victor, by telling him how to spell stickleback, and that whales weren't fish. He would have done better to keep his information to himself. If Victor had told him that his racing car had oval wheels he felt sure that he would have been offended, even though it was true.

All through the lunch hour he kept a look-out, hoping to catch sight of Victor's grin in the distance, but as usual he ended up walking round the playground by himself.

When school was over he began to walk home alone. Once out of town there was no pavement on the Pallingham road so he climbed the bank and teetered dangerously along the top of it, his feet on a level with the roofs of passing cars. After a few minutes he felt someone punch his foot, and looking down he saw Victor drawing alongside on a bicycle with handle-bars that rose so high in the air that Victor seemed to be dangling from them. Andrew slithered down the bank to the road and Victor scooted along beside him.

'Do you live out this way then?' said Victor.

'In Pallingham, yes,' said Andrew. 'We moved in last week.'

'You don't live in the Newmans' old place, do you?' asked Victor. 'Tiler's Cottage, back of the church?'

'That's it,' said Andrew.

'Well then, you're our next door neighbours, almost. We live down the loke.'

'Down the what?'

'Down the loke.'

'What's a loke?'

Victor looked puzzled. 'A loke's a loke. Don't you have lokes in Kent?'

'No, we don't. What is it, a hole?'

'How can that be a hole?' asked Victor.

'You said you lived down one,' said Andrew. Victor pointed across the road at a gap between two houses. 'That's a loke.' Andrew looked.

'It's a lane.'

'That's not. Lanes go somewhere, lokes stop halfway. I'll show you our loke when we get home. Fancy us being neighbours. What did you want to move up here for and come to our rotten old school?'

'What's rotten about it?' said Andrew. 'I've seen worse.'

'I hate school,' said Victor. 'No, I don't. I don't hate that. I just wish that was different.'

'You wouldn't wish it was like my last school,' said Andrew. 'I hated that. There was too many of us. I met our house master in the street one day and he didn't recognize me and that was after a whole term.'

'Everyone recognize me,' said Victor. 'Haven't you heard them? "Is that you at the back, Skelton? Stop talking, Skelton. Come you out of that toilet, Skelton." '

'Who's Skelton?'

'Me,' said Victor.

'At my other school half the teachers never knew our names,' said Andrew. 'I got caught down the boiler room one day and I was so scared I gave a false name. This teacher said "What's your name, lad?" and I said Graham Hill. It was the first name I could think of. I'd seen him the night before, on the television.'

'Did that teacher find out?'

'No; but there was another Graham Hill in the second year. He found out,' said Andrew, remembering what the other Graham Hill had done about it.

'I bet he was pleased,' said Victor. 'I bet he was. What were you doing in the boiler room?'

'It was better than going on the playground,' said Andrew. 'Everybody was in a gang. I wasn't in a gang. They said I talked stuck-up.'

'They must have talked horrible if you sounded stuck-up,' said Victor, frankly.

'I didn't realize then,' said Andrew, 'that you have to talk different at school than you do at home.'

'I don't,' said Victor. 'I swear a bit more at school than I do at home, but I reckon I sound the same, doing it.'

'Then I started talking at home like I did at school. I didn't notice but my Mum did. She didn't think much of it, I can tell you. I think that's one of the reasons we moved.'

'You never moved because of the way you were talking,' said Victor.

'It wasn't only that. Just after my brother was born Mum held him up and said, "He looks like a teeny weeny soccer hooligan already. It must be in the air, let's move." So we did."

'Is he a soccer hooligan?' asked Victor, with interest. 'Boots and that?'

'Of course he isn't, he's only eight months old,' said Andrew. 'Mum never says what she means. She says something different and you have to guess. We've moved seven times since I was born. I went to three junior schools and two secondary schools. This is the second.'

'Do you think you'll stop, this time?' said Victor.

'We might,' said Andrew. 'Mum and Dad like it here. I expect I shall, in the end.'

'I've always lived here,' said Victor. 'I wish I could go to a different school every term. I wouldn't get bored then.'

'You'd never learn anything.'

'I never learn anything anyway,' said Victor. 'Everybody read better than me. Everybody write better than me. I'd like to join the Airforce when I leave school, but I don't reckon they'd have me. Maybe I'll drive a tractor, like my Dad. What do your Dad do?'

'I don't know, quite,' said Andrew. 'He works with computers. We've got all this paper tape at home, full of holes. It looks as though you ought to be able to do something with it but I can never think of anything. Mum made paper chains out of it, last Christmas.'

'Do your Mum work?'

41

'She used to,' said Andrew. 'She stopped when she had my brother: now she says she'd like to go back, just for the rest. She worked in a library.'

'Books and that? Is she clever then?' asked Victor, suggesting both admiration and disgust.

'Books? You should see our house,' said Andrew. 'We've got thousands, all over the place. I'll tell you, when we move, the first thing that gets unpacked is the books. Then Mum starts reading them and nothing else gets unpacked. We came here a week ago and we haven't even got the curtains up yet. All the books are out though, all over the floor. You can't move.'

'We've got some books,' said Victor. 'Three or four. Do you like reading?'

'Sometimes,' said Andrew. 'Technical manuals and magazines. I don't like reading books unless they're funny.'

'I read so slow I can't tell what's funny and what isn't,' said Victor.

When they reached the church Victor stopped.

'There's a short cut here, round the back. I don't usually use that when I've got the bike but if you give me a hand over the wall we'll go that way.'

They went through the churchyard the way Andrew had done on his first morning, but instead of using the gate on the far side, Victor led the way round behind the yew trees to a place where the graves were so old and mossy they were sinking back into the ground. Victor sat himself astride the wall.

'There's a big drop on the other side,' he said. 'I'll go over first and you lower the bike down to me.' He dropped out of sight and Andrew, looking over the wall, saw him land, eight feet below, knee-deep in what looked like pea-plants. He lifted Victor's bicycle and heaved it over the wall. When Victor stretched up and took hold of it from beneath, Andrew followed it. The drop looked much more than eight feet while he was hanging by his hands from the top of the wall, and he felt like going back until he noticed that although his head was eight feet above the ground his shoes were five feet lower, so he let go and dropped, landing beside Victor.

'They are peas,' he said, as he picked himself up. 'Aren't they funny? I've never seen them so small. I thought they always grew up sticks.'

'Those go for freezing,' said Victor, wheeling the bicycle away under the shadow of the wall. They were walking on a little, greasy mud path and the pea-plants trailed across it. The pods went off like detonators under their shoes. 'They aren't picked by hand. They have to be small for the machines to pick them.'

When they came to the end of the wall, Victor struck out across the pea field, and there was a perfect salvo of exploding pods.

'Shouldn't we stay on the path?' said Andrew, looking round, warily.

'This is the path,' said Victor. 'That have to be ploughed in, every year and they set the crop over it. We can still use that. I think I'm the only person who do use it, that's why that don't show up.'

At that moment there was a terrific explosion, just behind them.

'We're being shot at,' cried Andrew, convinced that they were trespassing after all. He looked round for the gunman.

'That's the old bird-scarer,' said Victor, pointing to a machine that squatted among the pea plants a few yards away.

'It looks like a little cannon,' said Andrew, still twitching.

'Well, that is, really,' said Victor. 'That work off bottled gas. There's another one, down there. Don't worry, that won't go off again for a bit. Haven't you heard them before?'

'Yes, but I thought it was a gun. There's a man goes past our house, every night. He's got a gun.'

'That'll be my Dad, out after pigeons,' said Victor. 'We have them for supper.'

'You eat pigeons?' said Andrew. Pigeons were pets: it was almost as bad as eating guinea-pigs.

'This is the loke,' said Victor as they came out of the pea field and through a gap in the hedge. 'That's our house, half way down. I'd ask you in but my Mum like to know if we've got anybody coming.' He turned in at the gate. 'I'll probably see you on Monday,' he said, as he scooted up the path. Andrew saw a cross face looking out of the window and hurried on, round the corner, into his own lane.

Towards Tiler's Cottage he overtook Mum, pushing Edward in the pram. Edward, with a gentle smile on his face, was strangling a banana.

'Where did you spring from?' said Mum. 'I thought you'd be home already.'

'I walked home with a friend,' said Andrew. 'He lives down the loke.'

'What's a loke?' said Mum, pleased that he had a friend, but not saying so.

'Half a lane,' said Andrew.

5 | Victor Ludorum

He didn't see Victor again during the weekend, but it felt friendly just knowing that it was Victor's chimney that he could see from the landing window and that the gunman was Victor's father, even though he was going to shoot pigeons and looked as if he would like to be shooting people.

'Pigeons are vermin,' said Dad, when he mentioned it. 'They destroy thousands of pounds worth of crops. I don't think you'd be very popular if you kept them as pets round here.'

'I shouldn't fancy cooking them so you needn't go and shoot any,' said Mum. 'Feather pie and claw pudding. There can't be much meat on them.'

'Oh yes, there is,' said Dad, who had lived in the country as a boy. 'Not surprising, really, when you consider what they stuff themselves on all the year round. Perhaps I'll get a gun as well.'

'You'll shoot your toes off,' said Mum. 'I won't cook them, that's for sure.'

'Can I ask Victor here sometimes?' asked Andrew, afraid that he would be squeezed out of the conversation as he so often was when both his parents joined in.

'Whenever you like,' said Mum. 'He sounds interesting.'

'He sounds like The Archers,' said Andrew. 'Sort of. But real instead of pretending.'

'Oh,' said Dad. 'A local man, is he? Perhaps he can show us around. I got lost coming back from the garage today when I went for petrol.'

'I got lost going out,' said Mum. Andrew saw that he was going to lose the conversation again and gave up. He went out to see the guinea-pigs.

On Monday and Tuesday he walked home with Victor, but they rarely met in school. On Wednesday Victor said, 'Tomorrow is Sports Day. Are you in anything?'

'Not me,' said Andrew. 'I haven't been here long enough. Anyway, I'm no good at games. I never got into any teams at my last school. I put my name down for the Under Thirteen Cricket but nobody else did, so there was no team to get into. One boy stuck a javelin through his foot, just before I left. I think he was going to stick it in someone else but they moved.'

'I'm going in for everything,' said Victor. 'I'm no good either, but that's a laugh. You shout for me, won't you, when I break my neck in the high-jump?'

Andrew found himself alone for Sports Day. He sat in the spectators' enclosure, being trampled on every time a new event was called. There was a certain amount of confusion because a strong wind was blowing and it was difficult to hear what was being said over the public address system, which whined and hooted every time it was used. Important announcements were drowned by the noise of passing aircraft, which kept up a steady reconnaissance all afternoon.

People stood in front of him, fell over his legs and walked on his coat. He kept an eye on the score board to see how his house was doing, but it was always at the bottom. There were four houses: Browne, Nelson, Paston and Crome, all named after famous Norfolk people. At least he supposed they were famous. He had never heard of any of them except Nelson but from reading an old school magazine in the library he had gathered that Browne was a doctor, Crome was a painter and Paston wrote letters. Letter-writing seemed a chancy way of becoming famous. Nelson was famous all over the country, so he was glad to be in that house although it was losing. Also, Nelson's house-colour was red, which was a good colour to wear. Paston were yellow; it had always struck him as a feeble sort of colour, but Paston were winning.

Victor was in Paston House, though if they were winning it wasn't due to Victor.

Watching him in event after event, Andrew understood for the first time what 'Lacks concentration' meant on a school report. It often appeared on his own but he was certain that he had never lacked as much concentration as Victor did.

He changed feet in the pole vault and direction in the high-jump. In the long-jump he seemed to hover in the air while deciding where to land which was never far enough from the take-off. His triple jump was a quintuple jump at the very least and his javelin twirled in the air like a drum major's baton, before landing, point up, behind him. Andrew waited to see him take off someone's head with a discus but when his turn came to compete, he was wandering about with his head tipped back, watching the fighters up above. No one told him: perhaps they were playing safe.

Andrew began to wonder if he were doing it on purpose. Wearing only a singlet and shorts, Victor

looked unprotected, as if he had gone into battle
without his armour. Possibly he felt unprotected too.
Anyone who habitually went about wearing four or
five layers of clothing was bound to feel at a loss when
he took them off. If he was allowed to compete in his
usual clothes he might sweep the field, winning every
event, if he weren't earthbound by the weight.

Then the mile race was announced.

It was an open race, the last on the book. Anyone
who still had the strength to put one foot before the
other was free to take part. The head boy himself was
there, in spiked shoes, doing flashy heel-and-toe
exercises on the sidelines. Then Andrew heard friendly
jeering and was startled to see the pale and ribby
figure of Victor doing similar exercises out on the
track. Andrew, in company with the rest of the
spectators, thought that Victor's starveling flanks
could never carry him round the first lap, let alone the
last three. He was ashamed to look as the competitors
lined up and the starting pistol was fired. Then he was
ashamed of feeling ashamed and made himself watch.

For three laps Victor was at the back of the field,
trotting in the rear with a mad, blank look on his face.
Two boys behind Andrew were betting each other
that Skelton would simply lie down and die before the
end of the race. Andrew began to pray, not to God but
to Victor, that he would at least stay on his feet.

On the last lap many of the runners began to fail.
The order of the day seemed to be that if you were
going to lose you lost spectacularly. People meandered
from one side of the track to the other, collapsing
decoratively among the crowd like marathon runners
entering the Olympic Stadium. Victor opened his

eyes, skipped nimbly round the bodies of the fallen, passed the head boy and came in third. The winner was in Nelson House but Andrew leaped up and down, cheering Victor, and was jumped on from behind by a Nelson supporter.

The mile was the last race so Victor came and sat sweatily with him during the prize-giving. The trophies were distributed by the Headmaster's wife and announced by the Headmaster with a megaphone, since the public address system had howled itself into silence. The wind was now so strong that his words were blown away behind him and several people walked off with the wrong prizes. There was a little fight at the back between the boy who had won the High-jump and the boy who had been given the cup.

Andrew watched long enough to see the winner win again and then turned to Victor.

Victor had hunched himself into a sweater and his anorak and was looking more at ease.

'Did you see those aircraft?' he said. 'I reckon they'd come to watch us.'

'How come you were third in the mile when you were so bad at everything else?' said Andrew.

'That take a long time to run a mile,' said Victor. 'I had time to think.'

'What did you think about?'

'I thought about how they were all expecting me to come last. They thought that was a joke, me running a mile,' said Victor. 'Old Skelton's soft in the head. Nothing between the ears. Brains in the feet. So I have, though, if that's what make me run.'

Andrew looked sideways at him and saw that his

everlasting grin was a little fiercer, a little less amiable, than usual. 'Were you angry, then?' he asked.

'I suppose I was,' said Victor. 'That's a good fuel, anger.'

6 | Flight Deck

Walking home at the end of the afternoon Victor said, 'Break-up tomorrow. You know we finish early?' Andrew hadn't known. 'Well, we do. We have lunch and the end-of-term service and we go home about half past two. My Mum said you could come over for the afternoon, if you like. Stay to tea, if you like.'

'I would like,' said Andrew. 'My Mum says you can come round to us any time you want.'

'Why don't you ask me, then?' demanded Victor.

'I wasn't sure you'd want to come.'

'Oh, yes. I like other people's houses, especially if they're dirty,' said Victor. 'Our house is too clean.'

'Ours isn't dirty,' said Andrew.

'I thought you said that was.'

'Untidy,' said Andrew. 'I said it was untidy. I didn't mean it was dirty. Well, it is, a bit. But it's not absolutely filthy.'

'I like houses a bit dirty,' said Victor. 'They smell nice and warm.'

Andrew thought that this was rather an odd remark, until he arrived at Victor's house on Friday afternoon. Friday morning was spent in tidying up, and the end-of-term service was soon over. It was easy to spot the people who were leaving. The girls wore a lot of make-up, collected autographs and cried in the cloakroom. The boys went round shaking hands with all the teachers they disliked most and lit cigarettes before they were out of the gate. Victor gave Andrew a lift on the back of his bike and they wobbled to a halt outside his gate just before three o'clock.

Victor parked the bicycle and went into the conservatory, making a great deal of noise wiping his feet. Andrew thought it wise to do the same. From the doorway, Victor's house had an unpleasantly shiny look about it and smelt like a dentist's waiting room. He began to see why Victor liked dirty houses.

Victor's mother was in the kitchen. She didn't say hello, she said, 'Don't make a mess on the floor, I've just cleaned it.'

Victor said, 'We've wiped our feet. Mum, this is Andrew Mitchell.'

Andrew said, 'Good afternoon, Mrs Skelton.'

Victor's mother said, 'You can't play in the lounge, I've got the vacuum cleaner in there. Mind where you're walking. I've just polished that bit.'

The kitchen floor was laid with white tiles. There were a few black ones, here and there. Andrew thought that it might have been better the other way round.

'I came third in the mile,' said Victor.

'Not in those shoes, I hope,' said his mother. 'You'd better go on up to your room. I'll call you when tea's ready.'

Victor set off across the kitchen, using the black tiles as stepping stones. Andrew followed him. The black tiles were a long way apart.

The lounge carpet was also white with a little bit of linoleum round the edge. They sidled round the lino like Ancient Egyptians and reached the door into the hall. Andrew was glad to see that the hall was tiled dark brown. There was a mat in it, but that was brown as well. He trod hard on the mat with both feet, although it wasn't in his way, and went upstairs, after Victor. Victor was going up bow-legged with his feet on the wooden bit at the side of the stair carpet. Andrew took off his shoes and walked up the middle. Victor's door was opposite the stairhead. With a mighty leap he cleared the landing and touched down safely in his own room.

'Shut the door,' said Victor. 'Nobody come in here, except me. I can do what I like in here.'

It was just like walking into a spider's web. Dozens of pieces of cotton hung from the ceiling and on the ends of the cotton were model aeroplanes. Andrew found himself nose to tail with a big Lancaster. Its rear guns were poking in his eye. He stepped back and charted a course across the room to where Victor was already stretched out on his back, half under the bed, staring up at a dog fight near the ceiling; two Spitfires and a Messerschmitt. Another Messerschmitt was sneaking round from behind the lamp-shade, but it seemed to have its sights set on a Hercules transport which was hanging from the light fitting itself. Andrew shoved his feet under the bed and lay down beside Victor. They stayed there, without speaking, for about five minutes, gazing at the aircraft.

From shoulder height, upwards, the walls were painted with stormy clouds, dark and choppy against an angry yellow sky. A crack in the plaster had been filled in white to make forked lightning. Andrew thought of Victor's awful fish pictures and asked, 'Did you paint that yourself?'

'Not the sky,' said Victor. 'That was there already. That was the wall. But I did the clouds myself. Sort of. I copied them.'

'Out of a book?'

'No, out of the window,' said Victor.

'I wouldn't call that copying,' said Andrew. 'It's real painting if you do it from real.'

'You ought to see that at night,' said Victor. 'I put the light on – bomber's moon – and open the window so that they all blow about. You get great big shadows on the wall. I lie in bed and make the right noises.'

'What noises?'

'Oh, machine guns and ack-ack and bombs dropping. Then my Mum, she bang on the ceiling downstairs and I have to pack up.'

'Do you do that every night?' asked Andrew. 'Don't you ever read in bed?'

'Can't read by that light,' said Victor. 'That's only fifteen watts. Anything else would be too bright.'

Andrew was thinking sadly of Victor, alone in his room, night after night, with only a fifteen watt bulb. Then he understood. 'Too bright for a bomber's moon?'

'Too bright for any moon,' said Victor. 'Look.'

He reached up and pulled the cord that was hanging by the bed. The light came on. The shade was a white glass globe, and it shone with a moony glow, even in daylight.

'See those dead flies at the bottom,' said Victor. 'Craters.'

Andrew found he was kicking something papery under the bed. He craned his neck to see what it was and saw dusty piles of magazines and comics.

'My library,' said Victor, scrabbling under the bed and pulling out two bales.

One was old copies of the *Airforce Review*, the other was comics. The front page of all of them dealt with the exploits of Steve Stone of 777 Squadron. Steve Stone flew Hurricanes and had two friends who also flew Hurricanes, though not so well as Steve did. The friends were called Bob Fisher and Tubby Smith. Bob had the kind of moustache that parrots could perch on and rarely said anything other than 'Bang on!' Tubby Smith looked as if he was drawn with a pair of compasses and had to be levered into his Hurricane every week.

The man who illustrated Steve Stone could draw aeroplanes but not people. All the men of 777 Squadron seemed to have been sawn off, just below the knee and wore their feet where you might reasonably expect their shins to be. This might not be a bad thing, thought Andrew, after looking through half a dozen episodes. Steve and Bob spent many flying hours clambering about on the fuselage or dangling from the landing gear. Having such short legs must lower their wind resistance considerably. Tubby, of course, had to remain jammed in his cockpit.

'Do you believe all this?' asked Andrew, pointing to a picture of Steve Stone flying his Hurricane under the Eiffel Tower.

'Of course not, but I bet you could. I bet you could fly a Hurricane under Yarmouth pier, if you tried,' said Victor. 'Have you seen Mitch Mulligan, the Wellington Wizard?'

He passed over a second heap of comics entitled *Action*, the name printed in exploding yellow letters on a red background. Andrew flipped through the top one, looking for someone in gumboots and a pointed hat. He found, however, that Mitch Mulligan was the ace mechanic of 999 Squadron who did such amazing things to the Wellington bombers in his care that they flew upside down, landed safely in deep water and even took off like Harriers from small vegetable gardens in Occupied France.

Mitch was drawn square and squat, because he was a mechanic. His neck was wider than his head and his hands were bigger than his feet. He always carried an adjustable spanner, even when he was doing delicate work in the instrument panel.

'I'd like to be an aircraft mechanic, if I couldn't fly,' said Victor.

'You're the wrong shape,' said Andrew. He was looking at a picture of Mitch leaping, like an agile toad, from the wing of his bomber. 'He looks like the Dambusters' bomb. I wonder they don't drop him, by mistake.'

'That's a terrific film,' said Victor. 'I could watch that over and over again. That and the *Battle of Britain*. All those little Spitfires whizzing about. Haven't you got any aircraft?'

'I've got racing cars,' said Andrew. 'Enough for a proper Grand Prix, but I can never find enough space to lay out a track.'

'Have you got them hanging up?' said Victor, not attending.

'They're cars, not aeroplanes,' said Andrew. 'What would be the point of hanging them up?'

'Don't you ever see any aircraft in Kent?'

'Sometimes, but you have to go looking for them,'

57

said Andrew. 'They aren't all over the place like they are here.'

Victor's mother looked in at the door and said, 'Tea's ready. Don't you bring any of that mess downstairs,' and went away again.

'I never take any of my stuff downstairs. Wouldn't dare, that might get clean. Come on, then,' said Victor, pushing his library back under the bed. He stood up and removed his anorak and one sweater, in preparation for the meal to come. Andrew withdrew his feet, picked the fluff off his socks and replaced his shoes. They tiptoed down.

The Skeltons did not eat their meals in the kitchen. There was a special room for that. Victor's father was home and sat at the head of the tea table, reading the paper with a frown that went up and down his forehead like a venetian blind. He took no notice of Andrew and Victor so they sat down and said nothing themselves. It was very difficult to talk with Mr Skelton in the room. While the tea was being poured, Victor attempted to make conversation.

'I came third in the mile,' he said.

'You told us that yesterday,' said his father.

'I thought you didn't hear, yesterday,' said Victor.

'He beat the head boy,' said Andrew. 'The head boy was fifth.'

'When you're head boy perhaps you'll come first,' said Victor's father to Victor. Clearly, this was the only kind of congratulation he was going to get.

Nothing else was said all through tea. It was a good meal, judged purely as a meal and not as a pleasant way of passing the time. At home, Mum, Dad and Edward would be having their tea, all over the kitchen and probably half way up the stairs as well. Andrew thought it was a nice change to have a meal with everything laid out on a table where you could see it, and on a cloth, at that; but he did wish someone would speak. The only sound was of jaws closing on food.

'Can we help with the washing up?' asked Andrew when it seemed as though everyone had finished eating.

'No,' said Victor's mother.

'Thank you,' she added, some seconds later. She began to clear the table. Victor's father stormed out of the room as though someone had insulted him, though Andrew didn't see how it could have been done as no one had spoken. He and Victor crept from black tile to black tile, across the kitchen and out of the back door. He noticed that Victor wiped his feet going out as well as coming in.

'Do you want to come back to my place?' said Andrew.

'Won't your Mum mind?'

'Why should she?' said Andrew. 'She might be surprised if you didn't.'

'Just for half an hour, then,' said Victor. 'I'd better be back before my Dad go out.' He said something else as well but Andrew didn't hear what it was. One of the fighters roared over the house, drowning every other sound. It was the same kind that Andrew had seen on the day they moved into Tiler's Cottage. He turned to the expert.

'What was it?' he asked, as soon as he could make himself heard.

'Phantom,' said Victor. 'Haven't you seen one before? They've been over a lot, lately.'

'I've seen enough of them, but I didn't know what they were,' said Andrew. 'Why do they fly here so much?'

'Maybe they like the view,' said Victor. 'There's usually four of them together.'

As he spoke, two more Phantoms, in muddy camouflage, swooped overhead.

'Wait for it,' said Victor. 'Here he come.' The last Phantom followed the first towards the coast, trailing a fat cloud of filthy smoke.

'I can hear a Lightning coming,' said Victor. Andrew could only hear the Phantoms going. 'Up there,' said Victor, pointing skywards. A little smudge of a plane was cruising between two clouds.

'How can you tell what it is?' said Andrew. 'Have you got telescopes in your head?'

Victor laughed. 'I can tell by the engines. Lightnings have Rolls Royce Avon turbojets. Phantoms have General Electric turbojets. They're American planes actually – made by McDonnel-Douglas. The Luftwaffe have those as well.'

Andrew stared at him, wondering how someone who pretended to be such an ignorant slob could possibly know so much or reel it off with such ease.

'Haven't you noticed how they howl?' said Victor. 'The Phantoms, I mean. The F-III sounds a bit like that as well. That's got turbofans; Pratt and Whitney. You don't see them so much round here and they never fly as low as the Phantoms.'

'What's an F-III?' said Andrew.

'Swing-wing tactical strike fighter,' said Victor, crisply. Even his accent had dropped away. He sounded like a teacher. Andrew thought that Victor might not care to be told that.

'General Dynamics,' Victor went on, executing a couple of swing-wing manoeuvres himself as they went through the gate. Andrew hurried after him.

'They all sound the same to me,' he said. 'Just a row.'

'Well, I dare say you could tell them apart by looking at them,' said Victor. 'You can always spot a Phantom by the Radar cone. They look like they've got a dewdrop on their noses. And their wings turn up at the tip. Bit like a Stuka.' Andrew looked blank. 'Bit like a rook.'

'Have you ever seen a Harrier?' said Andrew. 'Going up and down?'

'Not going up and down,' said Victor. 'But I often see them go by. I expect you have too but you didn't recognize them. Now they make a row. Rolls Royce Bristol Pegasus vectored-thrust turbofan.'

'I suppose you can recognize them as well,' said Andrew.

'Of course I can – but I've grown up to it,' he added, kindly, in case Andrew thought he was showing off.

Andrew did.

'I knew this boy at my last school, he used to do that with cars. He used to walk home with me sometimes and every time a car came up behind us he'd say what it was, before we could see it.'

'Was he any good?' asked Victor, jealously.

'He was right about half the time,' said Andrew. 'But he would make excuses when he wasn't right. We'd hear this car, see, and he'd say it was a Lotus Elan and then this horrible old Renault Dauphine would come round the corner and he'd say it sounded just like a Lotus Elan that needed its tappets adjusting or something daft like that. I got so sick of him I used to hide in the cloakroom and go home the long way.'

'I'd never do that,' said Victor. 'If I didn't know, I wouldn't say anything.'

'I didn't mean you were like that,' said Andrew. 'I was just wondering how you learnt it all.' He saw Victor's grin droop, slightly, at the corners. 'I didn't say I didn't believe you, I just thought you didn't like learning things.'

'I didn't learn them,' said Victor. 'I can't learn things, but anything I want to know sticks.' He still looked worried.

'Is that a Phantom coming now?' asked Andrew, fairly sure that it wasn't but hoping to cheer Victor up.

'That's a helicopter,' said Victor. The flying long-distance coach appeared above the trees. 'We get them going over all day. They go to the rigs.'

'North Sea Oil?' said Andrew. 'Oil rigs in the sea?'

'I don't know what rigs,' said Victor. 'But that's where they go.'

Behind the helicopter, but much higher, came another fighter.

'What's that then?' said Victor. 'Go on, have a guess.'

Andrew watched the aircraft rolling lazily through the clouds. 'Another Lightning?' he suggested, expecting to be wrong. Victor thumped his arm in delight.

'You've got it,' he said. 'Right first time. See, that's easy once you start.'

'I've seen a lot of them,' said Andrew. 'They go round and round all day.' He watched the Lightning until it was no more than a little dot, but by that time his eyes were full of dots and he didn't know whether he could see it or not.

'They come from Coltishall. R.A.F. Coltishall, that is. They're based there. You can stop at the end of the runway and they come in right over your head, yeeee-ow,' said Victor, making a screeching dive with the side of his hand. 'That's not far from here. We can go there, if you want. I do, all the time, in the holidays.'

'What do you do there?' asked Andrew.

'Just watch them,' said Victor. 'Just watch Lightnings all day long. You get a few other planes but they don't usually land, they just go overhead. I love Lightnings, they used to be the fastest plane in the world, one time. You ought to see them climb. They have re-heats.'

Andrew was afraid that Victor was becoming technical again. He had never heard of re-heats. It sounded like a disease. Good morning, Doctor. I'm ever so poorly, I've got re-heats. No cure for that, Madame, you'll have to have them out.

They had arrived at Tiler's Cottage. The front door was open so they went in that way. Victor was impressed.

'We never use our front door,' he said. 'I don't know anyone who use the front door, only old Mrs Hemp and she hasn't got a back door.'

Andrew went through to the kitchen. Mum and Edward were playing on the floor.

'Hello,' said Victor to Andrew's mother. Then he saw Edward. 'What's this, then? Is this yours? Is this your brother?'

Andrew had been afraid that Victor would despise the baby and despise Andrew for being related to him, but Victor knelt down on the carpet and picked him up, each fat hand in one of Victor's bony fists.

'His arms will come out of their sockets,' said Andrew, watching Mum out of the corner of his eye.

'No, they won't. Little gorillas can do this when they're born. He's just like a little gorilla,' said Victor. Edward dangled for a moment and then his arms tautened as he took his own weight and began to swing. 'He know what he's doing,' said Victor. 'What's your name, baby?'

'Edward,' said Mum.

'That's a funny name for a baby,' said Victor.

'He won't always be a baby,' said Andrew. 'I don't suppose you looked much like a Victor when you were born.'

'My Mum say I looked like boiled bacon when I was born,' said Victor.

'Most babies look like boiled bacon,' said Mum. 'You have to think ahead. I hoped Edward would suit him later on. I dare say he'll grow to fit it.'

Victor sat down and took Edward onto his lap. 'Haven't you got any teeth yet?' Edward took hold of Victor's finger, examined it thoughtfully, put it in his mouth and began to gnaw it.

'Watch out,' said Mum. 'He may not have any teeth but he'll give you a nasty suck.'

'Don't you gnash your gums at me,' said Victor.

Dad looked in at the door. 'I can smell burning. Have I left anything switched on?'

Mum looked round, sniffing. 'The soldering iron. You left it in the plate rack.'

Dad went over to the sink and picked up the soldering iron. Welded to the tip of it was a pink plastic egg cup. 'Very sculptural,' he said.

'I'd say something entirely different,' said Mum, prising the egg cup loose. 'What would your mother say, Victor?'

'No one would leave a soldering iron in our plate rack,' said Victor. 'That stays in the shed. So do the vice,' he added. Andrew looked and saw that their vice was clamped to the table with a piece of wood in it. Under the table was a sheet of newspaper, covered in shavings.

'Mum burned herself on one of my old teeth, once,' said Victor. 'When one of the big'uns came out at the back I put that on the hot plate to see if that would split. I wanted to see inside.'

'And did it split?' said Mum.

'Yes, but I didn't see that. Mum picked that up first and burned her fingers. She said I was mad. I didn't get that back,' said Victor. 'I couldn't try again, that was my last tooth.'

'I've still got a back tooth,' said Andrew. 'We'll toast that when it comes out.'

'Take that soldering iron away,' said Mum. 'Why don't you keep it on your desk?'

'If you remember,' said Dad, 'there is a baby bath full of books and old shoes on my desk.'

'Your books and your shoes,' said Mum swiftly, and took Edward off to get ready for bed. Victor looked as if he might want to help.

'Come and see the guinea-pigs,' said Andrew. The hutch was still in the garden, and Ginger was asleep on top of it. Andrew tipped him off and Victor helped carry the hutch indoors.

'Is that your cat?' said Victor. 'Isn't he nice? I wish we had a cat. My Mum would go mad if I brought animals indoors,' he added, with envy. 'What are they called?'

Andrew pushed the hutch under the sink. 'This one is King Kong,' he said, taking out the black guinea-pig.

'My favourite gorilla,' said Victor.

'This one's Fittipaldi. I call him that because he's fast, or rather, he used to be.' He lifted Fittipaldi onto the carpet. The guinea-pig began to amble round in circles, getting longer and longer as he went.

'He look like he need a roller skate under him to keep his middle up,' said Victor. 'What do Kong do?'

'He whistles,' said Andrew. 'That's about all he does do. He isn't very bright.'

Victor stroked King Kong and tickled him behind the ears but he wouldn't whistle. He folded himself up, very small. Fittipaldi went under the vegetable rack, stole a runner bean and refused to come out. Andrew began to think that guinea-pigs were a boring waste of time and felt annoyed by the heaps of books, the pile of wood shavings and the vice on the table among the tea things.

'I wish our house was like this. I wish I could have a guinea-pig,' said Victor.

'Wouldn't you rather have a gorilla? You seem to know a lot about them,' said Andrew.

'First things first,' said Victor. 'Start with a guinea-pig and work up to a gorilla. Maybe no one would notice.'

7 | On the Polthorpe Road

Dad's holiday ended on Monday and he went off to his new job in Norwich.

'I suppose it's a bit like starting at a new school,' said Andrew, feeling complacent because his holiday was just beginning.

'Not really,' said Dad. 'I'm in charge and I'm the biggest. All the others are little chaps. I met them at the interview.'

Andrew went out into the lane and watched for traffic until the car had backed out of the garden and was safely pointed in the right direction. He waved good-bye and went back indoors. Edward was in his playpen in the kitchen, ripping up a newspaper.

'Litter-lout,' said Andrew, looking through the bars.

Edward gave a quiet, milky belch and smirked at him. He was full of porridge and all his problems were over until lunchtime. Mum came in and lifted him out of his paper nest.

'I've got a job for you,' she said to Andrew. 'Would you go into Polthorpe for the shopping?'

'All right,' said Andrew.

'Will you take Edward?' she asked. Andrew knew he was being told, not asked, but it was worth an argument although Edward was already being squeezed into his knitted coat.

'I can go quicker on my own.'

'There's no hurry,' said Mum, 'and if you take the

pram you can put the shopping on the tray, under-neath. It'll be heavy, I need potatoes.'

'I don't mind. I can carry heavy weights,' said Andrew. To prove it, he took the guinea-pig hutch into the garden, carrying it painfully under one arm. When he came back, Edward was in the pram.

'I don't want him here this morning,' said Mum. 'I'm going to clean the carpets. There will be a lot of dust.'

Andrew noticed several rolls of carpet stacked against the back door. None of them had fitted the last house and they had been rolled up for years. They were all off-cuts, bought cheaply in sales and they didn't look as if they would fit this house either. Mum unfurled one and took it into the garden to hang on the line. Andrew fetched a shopping bag and bumped the pram down the back steps. The carpet scraped his neck as he went by. It had green, furry pile on one side and something else green and furry on the other; not pile but growing. Andrew ran his fingernail down it and a little pale powder floated away. Mum came round the side of the house carrying an instrument made of cane, plaited and twisted into curious curves.

'What's that?'

'A carpet beater, very antique,' said Mum, flourishing it. 'I found it hanging behind the door in the coal shed.'

'I thought you were going to play tennis,' said Andrew.

Mum made a few practice strokes with the carpet beater. 'A rococo tennis racket,' she said.

'What's rococo?'

'With knobs on,' said Mum. 'With too many knobs

on.' She took a mighty swipe at the carpet and green powder came out in an evil cloud.

'The wind's blowing it away from the house,' said Andrew. 'If I put Edward round at the front he'll be well out of it.'

'You'll take him with you,' said Mum. 'You needn't be ashamed to be seen with him. Everyone was a baby, once. You were a baby, once. Attila the Hun was a baby, once.'

'What's he got to do with it?' muttered Andrew, but he could see that he had lost and ducked away before she could see him off with the carpet beater.

Andrew and Edward ignored each other for most of the journey. One chewed a piece of grass, the other, his collar. Then Victor, bulging with woolly pullovers, overtook them on his bicycle. Andrew couldn't hide the pram or pretend that it wasn't with him, so he pushed it with one finger, instead, as far away from it as he could get.

'How's my little gorilla, then?' said Victor, peering under the canopy. Edward jabbed at him.

'He's a thug,' said Andrew. 'Attila the Hun.'

Victor hadn't heard of Attila the Hun. 'Can I have a go?' he asked.

'What at?'

'The pram. Can I push the pram?' said Victor. 'You can ride the bike.'

Andrew was glad to swop.

'He's making a rotten old mess of his collar,' said Victor. 'It look like wet string.'

'It doesn't matter,' said Andrew. 'Mum won't mind so long as he doesn't swallow anything. You'd better look out for his button, it might come loose.'

'Your Mum don't mind what you do,' said Victor. 'Isn't she tall? I never knew a lady as tall as that. How tall is she?'

'I don't know,' said Andrew. All he knew was that he often wished she were shorter so that people wouldn't stare when they were out. He felt they were staring at him. 'She's taller than Dad and he's six foot,' he said.

'I'd like to be as tall as that if I wasn't a lady,' said Victor.

'You aren't, are you?' said Andrew.

'I mean,' said Victor. 'If I wasn't a lady I'd want to be – no, if I was a lady I'd want to be shorter than your Mum is. That's right.'

Edward felt neglected and began to grizzle.

'Shut you up,' said Victor. 'I'll sing to you. No, I better hadn't do that. Do you like nursery rhymes? I'll tell you a nursery rhyme.

> Little Miss Muffett sat on a tuffet
> Eating her curds and whey.
> There came a great spider
> And sat down beside her
> So she ate him, too.'

They stopped outside the supermarket in Polthorpe High Street.

'Go in and get your bits and I'll stay out here with Edward,' said Victor, neatly parking the pram between a basket on wheels and a pushchair.

'He'll be all right on his own. He won't choke,' said Andrew.

'Someone might take him.'

Andrew laughed. 'Who'd want him?'

'Someone might. Someone who wanted a baby

badly and hadn't got one. It do happen,' said Victor. He attached himself firmly to the pram by one hand and balanced the bicycle with the other. Andrew left him to it and went into the shop. He thought that if anyone wanted Edward badly it was Victor, but he didn't say anything. Victor didn't even have a guinea-pig. When he looked out of the plate-glass window between twin towers of tinned peaches, he saw that Victor had picked up a banana skin from the pavement and was flapping it just out of Edward's reach. They were both falling about, laughing.

When he came out, Victor flicked the skin away behind him and started bouncing the pram up and down.

'I saw you,' said Andrew.

Victor looked guilty. 'I didn't let him touch it. Anyway, that was all old and leathery. He couldn't get any germs off of that.'

Andrew let Victor push the pram home again and scooted beside him on the bicycle. As they left Polthorpe behind and followed the lonely road across the beet fields, dark clouds came up from the coast and hung over them. Threatening sounds came from inside the clouds.

'Thunder,' said Andrew.

'Lightnings,' said Victor.

'You can't hear lightning.'

'I said Lightnings, not lightning. Aircraft,' said Victor. 'Clean out your ears. You've got turnips growing in them. You couldn't hear a bomb drop. I thought I taught you what a Lightning sounded like.'

'It's all right for you,' said Andrew. 'If I had ears

like yours I could pick up radio waves.' Victor smiled. He was not vain about his ears.

Two grey aeroplanes came out of the clouds and dived inland.

'Going home,' he said. 'Coltishall. I'm going there, tomorrow. Do you want to come?'

'To the airfield? Don't you have to get permission?' asked Andrew.

'I told you, you can stop at the end of the runway if you like,' said Victor. 'You can't get inside – well, you can but you don't – but you can go almost anywhere you like, round the edge. I usually go to the firegates.'

Firegates sounded dangerous. Andrew didn't know what they were and didn't intend to ask.

'I'd like to come,' he said. 'If it's really all right.'

'Don't I keep telling you, anyone can watch as long as they stay outside the fence.' said Victor. 'Don't worry, we won't be arrested. That's not one of those places where you're not even allowed to stop.'

'When we were on holiday once,' said Andrew, 'we passed an airport where the runway was so short there were traffic lights on the road and when they went red all the traffic had to stop to let the planes go by.'

Victor wasn't listening. He seemed to have gone into a trance, thinking about Coltishall.

'I haven't been there since half-term,' he said. 'They don't fly at weekends.'

'What happens if war breaks out on a Saturday?' said Andrew.

'Leave a note, Come back on Monday,' said Victor. 'I went to the Open Day there, last year. That was terrific. They had Harriers there, and a Saab Draken, and Nimrod, and Hunters and a Victor. They even had a Vulcan.'

'What's a Vulcan?' asked Andrew. Come to that, what were Nimrods, Victors, Hunters and the Saab Draken? He was afraid to ask Victor too much in case he got a lecture on jet engines.

'Vulcans and Victors are V-bombers,' said Victor. 'At least they used to be. There still are Vulcans in service, but all the Victors have been converted to tankers for in-flight refuelling. They had Spitfires and a Hurricane, at the Open Day, I mean, and people jumping out of a Hercules transport.'

'Why?'

'With parachutes, of course. There's not going to be an Open Day this year. I suppose that's because of the fuel shortage.'

'They still have motor racing,' said Andrew. 'Look here, shall I have the pram back?' He didn't want to push it but he felt responsible for Edward's safe return. 'You keep shoving it up the middle of the road.' Victor took back his bicycle.

'I reckon racing cars use less fuel than jet bombers,' he said, weaving about among the cat's eyes like a skier on a slalom. 'Anyway, people pay to race cars themselves. Aircraft fuel come out of taxes, my Dad say. Last winter, when that petrol shortage was just starting, these four Phantoms came over and started doing loop the loops, just over there,' he said, pointing. 'My Dad was properly angry. He said it was a waste of fuel and someone ought to complain.'

'Did he complain?' asked Andrew.

'Not him,' said Victor. 'Well, only to my Mum. I made up a song about that.

Brightly shone the moon that night,
Though the frost was cruel.
When four Phantoms came in sight,
Wasting winter fu-hu-el.

'Was it at night?'

'Of course that wasn't. I couldn't have seen them if that was at night, could I? Just little red lights going blink-blink-blink-blink. I saw Phantoms at Bentwaters. That's in Suffolk. The U.S.A.F. have them in their aerobatic team.'

'What, like the Red Arrows?' said Andrew, glad to be able to drop a name himself.

'Red Arrows use Gnats. The Phantoms are the Blue Angels. Oh, you should see them go. You wouldn't think those dirty big Phantoms could move so fast. Blue Angels, Red Arrows, Blue Eagles, Pink Elephants...'

'I've seen the Red Arrows on the telly. Look out, there's a tractor coming. Is there really a team called the Pink Elephants?'

'No,' said Victor. 'There ought to be, though. They could use Dakotas. I've seen them at Norwich Airport. They're so old their wings flap.' He let go of the handlebars and spread his arms, wobbling along in the gutter, imitating a DC3 trying to take off in a high wind.

The tractor passed them rather closely, and Victor fell off, into a drainage ditch. Edward, who had been asleep, woke up and wallowed about in the pram, making angry, whirring noises.

Victor looked in at him. 'This baby will self-destruct in five seconds,' he said.

8 | Firegate Four

Tuesday was a day for staying at home, grey and windy. When Andrew got up it already looked worn out, like five o'clock in the evening at eight o'clock in the morning. Mum was in the airing cupboard, looking for a jumper that would still fit Edward.

'Do you think it's always like this up here?' she asked, as Andrew went by. 'I've never known such a miserable summer. Are you still going plane-spotting?'

'I suppose so. I don't even know how we're going to get there, yet. By bus, I expect. Victor didn't say.'

After breakfast Victor appeared at the gate with his own bicycle and another for Andrew.

'You can ride a bike, can't you?' he said. 'I never thought to ask. That's my brother's. He's in the Navy.'

It was a very long bicycle, like a greyhound. Andrew wasn't even sure if he would be able to reach the pedals.

'What'll your brother do if I bust it up?'

'He'll bust you up, that's what,' said Victor. 'You'll be all right with practice.'

Andrew approached Victor's brother's bicycle from behind, in case it shied, and made an experimental turn or two in the lane. Victor leaned against the gate, making minor adjustments to his shirt cuffs – all four of them.

'How big's your brother?'

'Like my Dad. Six foot three up and down and two

76

yards round. He look like a fork-lift truck when he shake hands. Take your arm off at the shoulder. Terrible temper,' said Victor. 'No, he's not. That's my sister Cheryl. My brother's a little fellow. Come on, you won't bust that up.'

'Are you sure about your brother?'

'His bark's worse than his bike, hey, that's a good'un,' said Victor. 'I didn't mean to say that. That said itself.'

When they got to the end of the lane Victor turned left instead of right.

'I know a short cut,' he said. 'That'll save going through the town.' He meant Polthorpe which Andrew had taken for a village. Compared to Pallingham, it was a city.

By the time they reached the main road, Andrew felt confident enough to take one hand off the handlebars. He wanted to put it in his pocket, but after trying that he left it dangling outside in case it was needed in a hurry. Victor, on his bicycle, was so much lower down that he had to stand on the pedals in order to make himself heard above the noise of passing lorries. Andrew was glad when they reached a junction and Victor signalled to turn right into a minor road.

'We'll go cross-country,' he said. 'We'll go through Sloley.'

'Go through what, slowly?'

'Sloley,' yelled Victor. 'That's a village.'

'I thought you mean slowly, like – major road ahead.'

'How can you ride a head?' said Victor. He was having a witty morning.

When they reached the next cross-roads Victor dismounted and scanned the sky, above and behind.

'Nothing up yet,' he said. 'That's too early for them. Still having breakfast. I hope that don't rain. They don't like getting their Lightnings wet.' He held up his finger to test the wind, although Andrew thought it was quite obvious that it was coming from the left. 'That's in the South. Ought to clear up, later.'

'Can you tell?' asked Andrew. Victor the countryman might know something about the weather that he didn't.

'That was on the weather forecast,' said Victor. 'Anyway, that's the best direction for us. They'll be taking off across the railway and landing right overhead, up at the other end. If they land over the railway you can't really get close enough. Hang on a bit. There's something up there now. I hear jets.'

'Lightnings?' asked Andrew.

'Naturally,' said Victor, nose in air.

They turned their faces to the wind and rode on until they came to a pub, painted pink and with an aircraft propeller fixed to the wall. Victor turned off the road and led the way down a lane.

'Nearly there,' he said, but Andrew could see no signs of an airfield. Tall trees grew on either side and there was no sound except for the wind blowing through them. They came to a war memorial and turned right again. By Andrew's calculations they should now be heading homewards.

'Here we are,' said Victor. Suddenly they came out into open country and Andrew saw buildings and pylons in the distance.

'Don't stop yet,' said Victor, pedalling faster. 'Wait

till we get to the lights.' They went on to a gap in the hedge and Victor braked without warning, throwing his bicycle into the hedge. 'There's one moving now, I think.'

They had stopped at a field of cabbages. Across the field, in straight lines, stood rows of lights on tall, yellow posts. Although it was daylight and the clouds were beginning to clear, Andrew found that it hurt his eyes to look at them.

'That's the approach to the runway,' said Victor. 'The road go through the middle of them. The rest are on the other side. Now look, do you see that tail?'

Beyond the lights they saw a metal shark's fin cruising above the cabbages. As it came closer, it was revealed as the stabilizer of a stocky grey aircraft.

'That's your Lightning,' said Victor, with love.

Andrew was disappointed. He had expected something sleek and elegant. In spite of the dull thunder of its jets, it seemed to have nothing to do with the roaring comets that streaked over his house every day. Except for the roundels and squadron flashes it was unpainted, its metal body not gleaming but leaden. It looked like a rather bad model of an aeroplane made out of bits of cardboard and the inside of a toilet roll. He was about to say as much to Victor when the Lightning reached the end of the runway and turned itself end-on to them. The sudden eruption of sound left him unable to say anything at all. He caught a brief sight of the two exhaust vents, one above the other and then the Lightning vanished.

He shouted, 'Where's it gone?' and Victor mouthed back, 'Down the runway. You'll see it in a minute.'

The stink of burning fuel oil rolled back to them

across the cabbages, and the rows of lights swayed and buckled in the hot air. In the shivering distance Andrew saw the Lightning shoot up and up over the horizon until it was no more than the familiar grey streak which was all he had known of Lightnings, until now. Unnoticed, another had come on to the runway and before the first was out of sight the second was soaring behind it.

'Wasn't that something?' shouted Victor. 'Wasn't that?'

Andrew dug his fingers into his ears and riddled the noise out of them.

'Do they meet in the middle?' said Victor.

'The ground shakes,' said Andrew. 'You can feel it shaking.'

'Shook you, didn't it?' said Victor. 'I bet you weren't expecting that.'

'They're funny little things on the ground, aren't they?' said Andrew.

'What do you mean, funny? What do you mean, little? They aren't little,' said Victor. 'They've got a wing span of thirty four feet, ten inches. They're fifty five feet, three inches long and nineteen feet, seven inches high.' Andrew cut him short.

'The only aircraft I ever saw close to were airliners,' he said. 'I mean, it is small compared with one of those.'

'Well, that's not a Boeing 747,' said Victor. 'Do you know, a Lightning can climb to forty thousand feet in two and a half minutes?'

'What happens now?' said Andrew.

'Not anything, for the moment,' said Victor. 'But sooner or later they'll be in to land. You remember, I said there were some up there, earlier. They'll land soon. Practice landings, that is. They don't come right down each time, that wear out the tyres too fast.'

Over to their right two planes broke out of the clouds and swung in a spacious circle, heading for the runway.

'They won't be down this time,' said Victor. 'They haven't lost enough height.'

'I bet you say that every time,' said Andrew.

'One more turn, then they'll be down,' said Victor, calmly. He knew.

The two planes passed overhead and sheared off for a second circuit.

'Losing height, I told you,' said Victor, revolving slowly to keep the Lightnings in view.

The second dropped back a little as the first completed its turn and aimed itself at them, rocking itself into position over the central row of lights, on the far side of the road, and then boring down onto the runway. Andrew drew in his head as it went over them and he looked up but saw nothing, only that darkness had passed for a second between him and the sky.

Victor, unshaken, stood on his toes and reported, 'It's going up again,' and the Lightning, which had momentarily vanished below the line of cabbages, reappeared. Behind it, two bright flares showed in the exhaust vents.

'It's on fire,' Andrew shouted. 'It's going to crash.'

'Those are the re-heats,' said Victor. 'Now, you watch that go up,' and the aircraft stood on its tail and climbed into the clouds. There was no time to watch it, it had gone.

'But it's burning,' cried Andrew.

'That's not,' said Victor, and Andrew knew, for a moment, that he had hoped it was: not that he wanted to see anyone killed but it would have been a fine sight, something so large and powerful, burning across the sky.

The second Lightning came down over their heads. Ready for it this time, Andrew saw the lettering underneath, the flaps, the wheels, the landing lights. Victor was jumping about, trying to see whether it had landed or not.

'That's down. That's landed. No, it hasn't. That's going up again.'

And again Andrew saw the red flares and smelled burning.

'That's all right,' said Victor, noticing him stare. 'They're meant to do that. That make them go faster. That's only fuel burned in the exhausts.'

Andrew said nothing. It was the same feeling that he had had at Brand's Hatch, hoping that something would happen and not liking to think what it was: pretending that he wasn't hoping at all.

'Let's go round to the firegate,' said Victor, who thought that Andrew was nervous. 'That's not so exciting, but you get a better view if they do land.'

He took his bicycle out of the hedge and started back the way they had come. Andrew followed him.

They returned to the main road, riding between fields of cows and fields of wheat, keeping the airfield in view, in the distance. When they reached trees and houses Victor turned back, down a lane so narrow that only one car at a time could have passed along it and grass grew in the middle on the part where no wheels ever ran. The airfield was out of sight again, behind the trees. In the little, rutted lane, there was no way of knowing that war planes took off and landed a hundred yards away. They passed a farm and a field where three quiet horses looked over the hedge and it was a shock to hear Victor say, 'That's it, up ahead. Firegate Four.'

Firegate Four, after all, was just a gate. It stood across the end of the lane, on one side farmland and cottages, on the other, the airfield. It was surrounded by notice boards of a discouraging kind.

MINISTRY OF DEFENCE
PROPERTY

KEEP OUT
EMERGENCY EXIT NO.4
KEEP CLEAR

and on the gate itself:

KEEP CLEAR
FIRE FIGHTING VEHICLES
WILL CRASH THROUGH THIS
GATE IN EMERGENCY

Victor got off his bicycle and leaned it against the fence. It was no more than a row of palings, wired together like an ordinary garden fence, but the gate was meshed over and topped with barbed wire.

Andrew thought that Victor was being rather casual.

'We shouldn't be here, should we? Won't someone turn us off?'

'Everyone come here,' said Victor. 'This bit is sort of the car park.' He indicated a cindery patch of ground beside the gate, engraved with tyre tracks. Andrew was not convinced.

'I bet someone's watching us. We might be spies for all they know.'

'There's nothing here to spy on,' said Victor. 'If there was we'd be moved on, fast enough.'

'You can go to prison for this, in some countries,' said Andrew.

'Yes, but not here. Look, nobody care if you watch the Lightnings, they've been around for years. I can't remember when they weren't,' said Victor. He climbed onto the firegate.

'It says fire fighting vehicles will crash through it in an emergency,' said Andrew.

'I reckon I'll see them coming,' said Victor. 'I can read words six inches high, you know. Those notices are to stop people parking their cars in front of the gate.'

Andrew climbed up beside him.

'You think I'm an idiot, don't you?' said Victor.

'No,' said Andrew. 'I'm sorry.' He knew he kept hurting the feelings that Victor pretended not to have. He decided only to ask questions, taking care not to argue with the answers.

Opposite the gate lay the runway. They were looking across it now, instead of down it. Beyond the runway were high buildings which Andrew took to be hangars.

'Are those hangars?' he asked.

'Those big sheds? Yes,' said Victor.

'What about that thing that looks like a blender?'

'A blender? So it do,' said Victor. 'That's the control tower.'

In front of the hangars the Lightnings stood in a row and little figures climbed over them. The fire engines waited expectantly in a building on the right.

'What happens if a fire engine meets a tractor in that little lane?' said Andrew.

'You'd see that tractor move, I reckon,' said Victor.

Andrew looked up and down the runway. At either end a Radar scanner revolved watchfully.

'Something's coming in now,' he said. Over the end of the runway, where he and Victor had stood earlier, a bright light hung in the sky. 'It's burning.'

'You and your burning,' said Victor. 'You'd like to see a fire fighting vehicle crash through me in an emergency, wouldn't you? That's the landing light on a Phantom.'

'So it is,' said Andrew, recognizing the trail of dirty smoke that drifted behind the aircraft. 'The lights didn't look so bright on the Lightnings.'

'Phantoms have bigger lights,' said Victor. 'That won't come down, they never do.' The Phantom didn't come down. It passed over the airfield about four hundred feet up.

'There's a Lightning coming in behind it,' said Andrew. The Lightning did land. That is to say, it sat down abruptly on the runway and little puffs of smoke spurted up round its tyres. As it raced by them a fragile parachute cracked open behind it and it began to lose speed. Before it reached the end of the runway it had stopped and the parachute dropped to the ground like a discarded skin. The Lightning took itself off round behind a barrier of concrete screens and a Land Rover dashed out onto the runway to retrieve the parachute.

'Do they always need a parachute? Was that an emergency?' asked Andrew, when the noise had followed the aircraft behind the screens.

'They'd go straight off the end of the runway without it,' said Victor. 'That's like a crash landing every time.'

'Dangerous,' said Andrew as the Lightning drew level with them again, heading in the opposite direction, towards the hangars.

Victor gaped at him.

'Of course that's dangerous. They don't do this for fun, you know. This is Strike Command. This is real.'

'But what do they do? We're not at war,' said Andrew, forgetting his resolution not to argue.

'Sometimes,' said Victor mysteriously, 'people need seeing off the premises.'

'What premises? You mean the airfield?' said Andrew. Fifteen jet fighters seemed a trifle excessive for the job.

'Not the airfield. Airspace,' said Victor. 'If foreign planes come into our air that shouldn't be there, they have to be seen out again. Lightnings are interceptor fighters. That's what they do. Intercept.'

They stayed at the firegate for another hour. Two more Phantoms passed by and three Lightnings landed. By this time several cars and a motor bike had joined them. People gathered at the fence and made ignorant remarks about the aircraft. Up on the gate with Victor, Andrew felt informed and superior.

'Getting crowded, isn't it?' said Victor. 'Let's move on.' They rode away, down the lane. 'Not enough aircraft and too many thick people,' he said. 'That fat fellow with a loud voice, he couldn't tell the difference between a Phantom and an F-III. If I didn't know that much I'd keep my mouth shut. Pity we didn't see any take off. You get the best view of all from there.

They leave the ground right in front of you. Do you want to go back to the other end and see if anything else turn up?'

'Anywhere you like,' said Andrew. Victor was in charge. Victor, who could just about read and barely write, knew more about aircraft than grown men with field glasses.

As they cycled along the main road they heard the sound of a prop-driven engine, over the airfield. Victor jumped off his bicycle and ran to the fence, leaving Andrew to stagger to a halt behind him.

Above the trees, a little, blunt fighter plane was banking towards them. Andrew thought he had seen one like it before, though not flying.

'Spit!' shouted Victor.

'What? Why?' said Andrew, not understanding.

'That's a Spitfire,' said Victor, hugging himself. 'That's a lovely little Spitfire.'

The Spitfire, free of the trees, dipped and looped and circled above them.

'Look how he throw that about,' said Victor.

'You couldn't do that with a Lightning,' said Andrew, detecting a flaw in Victor's brand loyalty.

'You could if you had enough room,' said Victor, quickly. 'But you wouldn't need to. Perhaps they'll send the others up. There's other Spitfires and Hurricanes. They go all over the country to air shows, but we can see them anytime we like. They live here. Most people have to wait for special occasions.'

'Every day, could we see them?' asked Andrew.

'Not every day, but quite a lot. Even once a month's better than once a year. I didn't tell you before in case that didn't go up and you didn't believe me.'

'I'd have believed you,' said Andrew.

'You don't very often,' said Victor. This was too true to be contradicted.

A motorist, seeing them at the fence, stopped his car and got out to see what they were watching. They all stared up at the Spitfire and it made its final run right above them.

'Specially for us,' said the motorist, joking.

'That was,' said Victor. 'If they see you watching they often do a bit extra. I've even seen a Lightning flying upside down when there was a crowd at the firegate.'

The motorist didn't believe him.

'It's true,' said Andrew, supporting Victor, although he didn't know if it was true or not.

The Spitfire went down behind the trees for the last time and the motorist went back to his car.

'If it wasn't for those, you wouldn't be here. Never forget that,' he said as he closed his door.

Victor looked outraged.

'What on earth does he mean?' said Andrew.

'He mean the Battle of Britain, what we won,' said Victor, scowling after the car. 'Every time some people see a Spitfire they say, "If it wasn't for that you wouldn't be here." I do wish they wouldn't.'

'Well, they're right, in a way, aren't they?' said Andrew. 'If we hadn't won, things might have been a bit different now.'

'I know they're right,' said Victor. 'But I don't want to be told. I don't need to be told. That make you feel you should go round kissing their wheels or something. People like that, it would be a sight more use if they'd done something about all the Spitfires being scrapped. Spits and Hurricanes and Wimpeys and Lancasters, all gone. Those at Coltishall are practically the only ones left. Do you know, they've got a Lancaster here as well, and that's the only one left in the whole world that can fly.'

'Will we see it?'

'I never have,' said Victor. 'Not here. I saw that go over our house once, but they have to be careful with it, that being the only one. I saw that at Bentwaters last year, and I got the pilot's autograph.'

Andrew tried to look impressed.

'Just think,' said Victor. 'Just think how he must feel. That's the only Lancaster left in the world, and he fly it.'

9 | The Grave Fisherman

When Andrew told Dad about the Lightnings he said, 'You know, don't you, that they won't be there much longer. There was an article about it in the local paper. I saw it at work. The Lightnings are being replaced by Jaguars.'

'E-Types?' said Mum.

'Not that kind of Jaguar,' said Dad. 'These are fighters.'

Andrew wondered if Victor knew and wished that he had heard it from him and not from Dad.

'When is it going to happen?' he asked.

'Quite soon, I believe,' said Dad. 'I dare say I could find out, if you're interested.'

'It's all right. I expect Victor will know,' said Andrew.

He met him in the lane, a few days later.

'What's all this about Jaguars replacing Lightnings?' he said. Victor looked as if it were something that he didn't much want to discuss.

'Next year, I think,' he said.

'Dad said it might be sooner. He saw it in the paper,' said Andrew.

'Papers often get things wrong,' said Victor. 'When my auntie got married they had our name down as Skeleton instead of Skelton.'

'What are Jaguars like?' asked Andrew.

'Tactical strike fighters,' said Victor. 'Skinny things.

I don't know why they want them at all. They can't even go as fast as Lightnings, only about a thousand miles an hour, maximum. A Lightning can reach Mach 2.27 at forty thousand feet. That's more than twice the speed of sound.'

'Perhaps they don't need Lightnings any more,' said Andrew. 'Perhaps they're out of date. They wouldn't replace them if they weren't.'

'If they were out of date they wouldn't still be using them,' said Victor. Andrew thought he was defeating his own argument in some way, but couldn't quite see how. What he could see was that Victor hated to think of a time when there would be no Lightnings over Norfolk. They might be new to Andrew but Victor had grown up with them. He seemed to be fonder of Lightnings than he was of people.

'Come in and see the guinea-pigs,' said Andrew.

Ginger had lately taken to sitting in the patent, monococque guinea-pig pen, with the guinea-pigs. As he made no attempt to eat them there was really no reason why he shouldn't. The three of them were sitting in the sun, under the wire netting and too near the ground to feel the wind.

Victor stuck his long forefinger through the wire and stroked Ginger under the chin.

'I wonder if he's like that underneath,' he said.

'What? Ginger inside as well?' said Andrew.

'No, I mean, I wonder if he's got stripes on his skin. If all his fur came off, would there be a pattern on him, as well?'

'I shouldn't think so,' said Andrew. 'Your head isn't black, under your hair, is it?'

'That is if I don't wash it,' said Victor. 'Hello,

King Kong's waking up. The world's smallest gorilla.'

He stood up and went through a few gorilla-moves himself, leaping from foot to foot, beating his chest and searching his armpits for imaginary fleas. Mum watched him from the kitchen door.

'Have you been bitten?' she asked.

'He's being a gorilla,' said Andrew.

'I've found the percolator. Can gorillas drink coffee out of cups or do they need a trough?' said Mum. Victor thought she was offended because he had been performing rude gorilla acts in her back garden. He stood still, looking humble and polite.

'We'll have it in cups, please,' said Andrew. 'With biscuits. Can we take it up to my room?'

'Good idea,' said Mum. 'I'm putting up curtains. I don't want you two climbing up them and swinging from the lampshade.'

'Curtains?' said Andrew, as they went in. 'Oh my, we are getting posh, aren't we?' Mum seized the carpet beater and chased them upstairs with it. Andrew slopped coffee all over his shoes as the carpet beater whistled through the air an inch from hisheels.

'Do she hit you with that?' said Victor.

'All the time,' said Andrew. 'Night and morning, regular.'

'Lies, all lies,' shouted Mum, from the bottom of the stairs. 'I just give him the odd flick with a cat o' nine tails to remind him who's boss. He's about due for one now, I should think.'

They raced up the second flight, to the attic.

'There's coffee, all over the stairs,' said Victor.

'It'll dry,' said Andrew. Victor looked thoughtful. Andrew imagined he was thinking about the consequences of spilling coffee on his own stairs.

Andrew's attic looked very bare after Victor's flight deck. He hoped that Victor might admire the racing cars, or the frieze of old cylinder head gaskets pinned round the wall or even the wing mirrors screwed to the wardrobe, but he went straight to the window and looked out, searching for a Lightning that he could hear, but couldn't see.

'Why don't you do your project on aeroplanes?' asked Andrew. 'Why do horrible fish when you could do aeroplanes? You don't even go fishing.'

'I don't know,' said Victor. 'Yes, I do, though,' he added, after thinking hard for a minute. 'If I started doing that for school, I wouldn't be interested in them any more. I don't care about fish, so I don't mind doing them.'

'Why wouldn't you be interested in them at school?' said Andrew. 'I thought the whole point of the projects was to do something you liked.'

'Ah, yes,' said Victor. 'But it would be having to like aeroplanes instead of just liking them. Every time a Harrier went over I wouldn't be thinking, there go a Harrier, I'd think, there goes my project. Then I wouldn't want to look at it. School's like measles. That spread.'

'Well, then, why not just do it for you and not for school? We could do it together. I can do the words and you can do the pictures,' said Andrew. 'You can tell me what to write.'

'You'll probably have to do the pictures as well,' said Victor, grinning. 'I can do clouds, I can't do anything else. I know, I'll paint lots of clouds and you draw aeroplanes on them.'

'I can't draw aeroplanes either,' said Andrew. 'Not accurately. I can't draw anything accurately. I came bottom in technical drawing at my last school.'

'You drew that car in General Studies.'

'I made it up. It would probably fall apart if anyone tried to build it. One of us will have to learn to draw.'

'Not me,' said Victor. 'There you go, you see. Just like measles. As soon as you put anything down on paper you have to start learning something. I don't want to learn things, I'd rather just find out. I tell you what, we won't neither of us draw things. We'll cut them out, instead.' He took the latest number of *Action* out of his anorak pocket. 'We can cut Wellingtons out of Mitch Mulligan.'

Mitch Mulligan was in trouble this week. One of the air crew was an enemy agent in disguise and there was Mitch, trapped on the tail plane at six thousand feet.

'How did he get out there?' asked Andrew as the enemy agent sabotaged the controls with a filthy foreign smile across his jaws.

'I don't know. I missed that last week,' said Victor. 'There was a strike, or something. Look, there's a Dornier down at the bottom. Let's have that out now. Got any scissors?'

'Won't it spoil the story on the back?'

'That don't matter. I never read any of the others, only the Airforce ones. Who is it, anyway?'

Andrew turned the page. 'The Marvellous Mystico,' he read. 'The circus conjuror who became a goal-keeper with Midchester Rovers. His team's success seemed like magic.'

'Oh, him,' said Victor, disgusted. 'He's properly

daft. He take footballs out of people's ears during First Division matches. I'd cut him up even if he didn't have a Dornier on the back.'

Andrew fetched scissors and they cut out the Dornier, half a Heinkel and two bits of a Wellington that appeared in adjacent pictures and almost fitted together.

Victor tried to draw a Lightning on a piece of paper but it got out of hand and became wider and wider towards the tail.

'I can't see where I'm going wrong,' he complained. 'I know exactly what that should look like, but that won't come out on the paper. That remind me of something but I can't think what.'

'A bell tent?' said Andrew, looking.

'Watch it,' said Victor. 'That's not that bad.'

'Victor Skelton's Flying Bell Tent,' said Andrew. 'If we had some Sellotape we could stick that Wellington together, otherwise the bits will get separated.'

'Where can we keep them?' asked Victor. 'We ought to put them away somewhere or they'll get lost and turn up under the bed in six months time.'

'Dad's got some files in his desk,' said Andrew. 'I'll get one now.'

'Hadn't you better ask first?' said Victor. 'Won't you get wrong if he find that's missing?'

'Of course not. I'll tell him tonight when he gets home,' said Andrew. He went down to get the file. Victor followed him but hung about in the living room, not wanting to be associated with a theft. Andrew came back with the file and found him looking at the books.

'Are all these yours?'

'Most of them are Mum's. I told you she worked in a library,' said Andrew.

'Is that where she got them from, then?' said Victor. 'Are there any about aircraft?'

'No, I had a look the other night,' said Andrew. 'Isn't there a library round here?'

'There's a van,' said Victor. 'Come round about once a month, and there's a library in Polthorpe, but that isn't open every day.'

'Shall we go and have a look at it, they might have something,' said Andrew.

Victor put the pictures into the file and they went out, stopping at his house to collect the bicycles. When they reached Polthorpe they found that the library opened on Tuesday mornings and Thursday afternoons. Today was Wednesday.

'O.K.,' said Victor. 'Let's go to Norwich. They must have a library there.'

'Isn't it rather a long way to go for a library?' said Andrew.

'That won't take long,' said Victor. 'That's only about fifteen miles.'

'But supposing it's shut as well?'

'All right,' said Victor. 'We'd better go home again. There's nothing to do here. The shops are all shut this afternoon. It look like everybody's died, don't it?'

There were only two roads in Polthorpe. Both were empty and dusty. No cars or people were about, only Andrew and Victor and their bicycles.

'Let's go back a different way,' said Victor. 'I don't feel like going home yet. My sister's there. Let's go down to the staithe.'

'What's a staithe?'

'Boats,' said Victor. 'Boats tie up there. I don't know what that is, that's just called the staithe. That's on the broad.'

Before they had moved to Norfolk and Andrew had known it only as a bulge on a map, he had at least heard of the Broads.

'I didn't know there was a broad here,' he said.

'Polthorpe Broad,' said Victor. 'That's round the back of the station.'

Polthorpe Railway Station had no railway. It had become a coal merchant's yard and they cycled between high, black mountains, on gritty, black concrete. Where the line had once been there was a grassy track. As they rode along it they could see water through the trees and on it floated houseboats, motor cruisers and yachts. There were a lot of people about, sitting on the bank with loud radios or standing masterfully on deck with their feet apart.

'Look at them,' said Victor, with great scorn. 'Wearing those silly hats. They think they're on the Q.E.2. and then they get stuck under Potter Heigham bridge.'

They went on past the houseboats and the trees until they came to a quiet stretch of water cut off from the rest of the broad by a rope boom with oil drum floats. All along the bank sat silent men with fishing tackle. Victor and Andrew went by very quietly in case they were accused of frightening the fish. It was beginning to rain and the anglers put up large umbrellas, orange and blue. Victor took a black P.V.C. raincoat out of his saddlebag and put it on over all his other clothes. It failed to meet at the front by a good three inches.

They left the old railway line and followed a cinder path back to the church. Just before it joined the High Street it ran along the side of the churchyard. Looking over the fence they saw another multi-coloured umbrella, poking up above the top of a tombstone.

'There's somebody fishing in the churchyard,' said Andrew.

'Perhaps he's fishing in a grave,' said Victor.

'Perhaps he's mad, he must be mad if he's fishing in a grave,' said Andrew.

'I wonder what he think he'll catch,' said Victor. 'Let's go and have a look.' They propped the bicycles against the iron railings and went up the path from the main gate.

'He's behind that big stone that looks like a table,' said Andrew. 'Let's pretend we're just walking through and have a look as we go by.'

He tried to take in a quick glance as he sauntered past but Victor propped himself against the tombstone and stared.

The man under the umbrella was drawing a picture. It seemed not to be a very good picture. Andrew thought this might be because the man was drawing mainly with the side of his thumb. He had a little camp stool, a holdall and a folder with the name J.F. Coates stencilled on the side of it.

'Is that you?' asked Victor, pointing to the name. Andrew realized that he had been reading it, not staring.

'That's right,' said the man. 'John Coates.'

'Are you an artist?' said Victor.

The man looked out from under his umbrella.

'Not what you'd call an artist,' he said. 'I draw pictures for books.'

Seeing that Mr Coates didn't seem to mind being disturbed, Andrew went back and had a look at the drawing. All he could see was a cloud of thumb smudges with a white space in the middle that was about the same shape as the church.

Mr Coates looked at him.

'I suppose you think I can't draw,' he said.

'Yes,' said Victor.

'I can, actually,' said Mr Coates. 'It's meant to look like that. And now I suppose you think I'm boasting and making excuses.'

'Oh, no,' said Andrew.

'Well, I'm not,' said Mr Coates. 'Anybody can learn to draw. There's nothing very clever about that.' Victor looked at Mr Coates, then at his drawing, and then ran back down the path.

'Has he gone off in disgust?' asked Mr Coates.

'I don't think so. He can't draw at all,' said Andrew. Victor fetched the folder from the saddle bag and returned with it. He took out his drawing of a Lightning and held it out under the umbrella.

'What do you think of that?'

Mr Coates was an honest man. 'I think it's terrible,' he said.

'It's easy to see you're not a teacher,' said Victor. 'If you were a teacher you'd say, "That's awfully good, what is it?"'

'I know what it is,' said Mr Coates. 'It's an aeroplane, or rather, it has been at some time in its career.'

'A Lightning,' said Victor.

'I was beginning to guess as much,' said Mr Coates.

'It looks as though you tried to draw it from both sides at once. It isn't made of Perspex, you know.'

'Aluminium,' said Victor. 'I should think aluminium. My Dad said, in the war they used to collect aluminium saucepans and melt them down to make aeroplanes.'

'They collected them, all right,' said Mr Coates. 'But as far as I remember they didn't make them into aircraft. It was the wrong kind of metal.'

'What did they do with them, then?' asked Andrew.

'Probably melted them down and made more saucepans,' said Mr Coates. 'Look here, this beast wouldn't fly. It might float, it wouldn't fly.' He turned the picture on its side and drew three little drogues on the end of it. 'What does that remind you of?'

'A space capsule,' said Victor. 'Re-entry. Splash-down.'

'Different requirements entirely,' said Mr Coates, drawing a row of spiky waves underneath. 'If a cone was the best shape for an aircraft, aircraft would be conical.'

While he was speaking he made a little picture in the corner of the paper. It was tiny, an inch long, but when he lifted his hand they could see that it was a Lightning.

'You've drawn Lightnings before,' said Victor.

'I have,' said Mr Coates, 'so I know what ought to be there. You draw what you think should be there. I would suggest that, in future, before you draw a line you decide where it's going to end. Don't keep going until it looks as though it's time to stop. You'll always be too late.'

All the time his pen was making marks on the

paper. One after the other he drew a Spitfire, a Harrier and a Phantom, all tiny, but there was no mistaking them.

'You like aeroplanes, don't you?' said Victor. 'I thought artists drew ladies with no clothes on.'

'Not all the time,' said Mr Coates. 'When I'm in Norfolk I like to draw aircraft. Haven't you heard it said that Norfolk is the world's largest aircraft carrier? Now, you can see what all these planes are, can't you? They've all got something that makes them absolutely distinct from the others. How do you know this is a Harrier, for instance?'

'It's got big lugs,' said Andrew.

'What's lugs?' said Victor.

'Ears,' said Andrew, pleased to trip Victor with a word he didn't know.

'Oh, ears,' said Victor. 'Like me. I should have been called Harrier, not Victor. Victors have their engines in the wings. Harrier Skelton, that's me.'

'Exactly,' said Mr Coates. 'No one could mistake you for your friend here. You are quite a different shape. That's just chance, though. Aircraft are different shapes because they need to be. That's what you must look out for.'

'Like fish,' said Andrew. Victor made a fist at him.

Mr Coates was drawing a Victor just above the Lightning. He joined them together with a line of ink.

'That's refuelling,' said Victor.

'Is your book going to be about planes?' asked Andrew.

'It's not my book,' said Mr Coates. 'I'm doing half a dozen pictures for it. It's about priory churches in East Anglia.'

'What's priory?' asked Victor. 'Is that what they're built of? I thought churches were built of stone. This one is.'

'A priory was a kind of monastery; you know what that is, don't you? A priory church is one that was originally built as part of a priory. Very often, the church is the only part left.' Mr Coates rubbed his thumb against a piece of charcoal and went back to making marks on his own drawing.

'I think we'd better go now,' said Andrew. He was tired of standing in the rain and thought that Mr Coates was tired of talking to them. 'Thank you very much for telling us how to draw.'

'I haven't told you how to draw,' said Mr Coates, putting his head out from beneath the umbrella again. 'I've just warned you off guessing,' and he went back under the umbrella like a tortoise into its shell.

Andrew and Victor collected the bicycles, Victor examining his page of miniature aeroplanes.

'I'll have another go at drawing that Lightning when we get back,' said Victor. 'Now I know how that's done.'

'I thought you didn't like learning things,' said Andrew.

'That wasn't learning, that was just finding out,' said Victor. 'We found out quite a lot, didn't we? About drawing and aircraft and priories, though I've forgotten that bit. What a good thing the library was shut.'

. 'I liked that bit about Norfolk being the world's largest aircraft carrier,' said Andrew.

'I knew that already,' said Victor. 'But I didn't want to spoil it for him by saying so.'

10 | A Fine and Private Place

Next day they went through Polthorpe churchyard again, in the hope that Mr Coates would still be there, sheltering from the rain under his fishing umbrella. There was no sign of him at all except for a little patch of flattened grass where his stool had been. Without the umbrella there was nowhere to shelter but in the lee of the big tombstone that looked like a table.

'I like graveyards,' said Victor, crouching behind it. 'When I was a littl'un I used to play in Pallingham churchyard. I used to pretend the gravestones were little houses. The one I liked best was round the back where we go over the wall. That's a big one, with an iron fence round it, up to your knee, about, and there's five graves inside. I used to think that looked just like a bed with people tucked up in it.'

'I wish we could get into this one,' said Andrew, wiping rain off his neck.

Victor shrugged his collars higher round his ears. 'I reckon there's someone in there already,' he said, and stood up to read the names on the top. It took him some time. 'Thomas Sutton, also his wife Catherine also his wife Elizabeth. I wonder if he was married to them both at once.'

'Perhaps they're all in there,' said Andrew.

'There wouldn't be room,' said Victor. 'This bit's just the front hall, like. They must be underneath. I expect he's in the middle with one each side, catching it in both ears.'

Andrew tried to make out the dates but the stone was flaking and scabby with lichen.

'His son's under the next one,' said Victor. 'I think that must be his son. William Sutton, son of Thomas and Catherine.'

Andrew moved round him to the next stone.

'This one is William's son, Thomas again. I think they've got the whole row to themselves.'

They followed the Suttons, alternately Thomas and William as far as the church door. The last of the line broke with tradition. He was Albert, in a dry corner against the stonework of the porch.

'Right out of the rain, lucky old Albert,' said Victor. 'Let's go in for a bit That's not going to stop yet.'

The floor of the church was paved with gravestones, from West door to altar. Up by the pulpit they found the oldest Sutton of all but they couldn't read his name. All the words except Sutton, which was writ large, had been worn away by passing feet.

'I shouldn't fancy to have people walking about over me when I'm dead,' said Victor.

'You wouldn't know anything about it,' said Andrew.

'Yes, I would. I'd come up and bite their feet as they went by. I'll be the famous ghost of Pallingham. People will come and photograph the grave and there'll be a little smudge down near the bottom of the picture and that'll be me, whipping back, inside,' said Victor.

'I don't believe in ghosts,' said Andrew, looking over his shoulder at a dark corner behind the organ. 'Dead people can't do anything.'

'They can, though. Didn't you ever see *'The Beast from the Pyramid?'* said Victor. 'That was on the television one night. My Mum and Dad went out and I came downstairs and watched that with my sister. She got scared and put all the lights on, even in the bathroom.' Victor sat down in a pew and stretched out his legs. 'There was this man, see, he was the Beast, who died millions of years ago and when this explorer came and opened up the pyramid, this man, the Beast, that was, came out of his box all wrapped in bandages.'

'But that's not true,' said Andrew, who thought that Victor should not be telling ghost stories in church. 'It never really happened.'

'I've seen pictures, at school,' said Victor. 'These people, they used to wrap up dead bodies to stop them going bad.'

'I know,' said Andrew. 'It was the Ancient Egyptians, but it wasn't millions of years ago. And it wasn't winding them up that stopped them going bad. They used to take the inside out and put something else in, instead.'

'Sage and onion?' said Victor.

'Don't be daft,' said Andrew. 'Spices and that.'

'Sage and onion isn't any more daft than spice,' said Victor. 'They weren't going to cook them, were they? Anyway, all the explorers had gone back to their tent and this lady come out in her nightie and go flapping about all over the pyramid.'

'Why did she do that?'

'I don't know. Not for any reason, I don't suppose. There wouldn't have been any more story if she hadn't. Ladies,' said Victor, 'always wear nighties in that sort of film. Anyway, just as she get to the end of this passage the Beast come out in his bandages, round the corner, and all the lights went out.'

'In the pyramid?'

'No, our meter ran out of money and the television went off as well and we couldn't find any more money in the dark. That was because of my sister having all the lights on. She wouldn't get off the settee in the dark. I had to go looking for tenpence to put in. She was too scared to move. I reckon she thought the Beast was in the kitchen waiting for her. By the time I found her purse the film was over and the adverts were on. I never found out what happened.'

'I've seen mummies in a museum,' said Andrew. 'Some of them were unwrapped. They were ever so little, not like real people at all.'

'Let's do a project on Mummies,' said Victor. 'We could make one ourselves.'

'Who are you going to use?' asked Andrew.

'I didn't mean a real one,' said Victor. 'Though I can think of a few people I wouldn't mind seeing wrapped up. Jeannette Butler, for one,'

'I'd rather stick to aeroplanes now we've started,' said Andrew. 'The library's open today, isn't it? Let's go across and see if they've got any books.'

'They should have,' said Victor. 'Seeing as that's a library.'

The library was a clanging tin shed behind the church. The lady librarian gave them each an application card and told them to have it filled in by their parents.

'My Mum's out,' said Victor. 'You'll be shut before I can get back again. I don't want to wait till Tuesday. Can't we take some books with us now?'

'What's the hurry?' asked the librarian. 'I know you, Victor Skelton. You've lived here for twelve years and this is the first time you've set foot in the library. It won't hurt you to wait a few more days.'

'My Mother used to work in a library,' said Andrew. 'Couldn't you trust us?'

'It's not a matter of trust,' said the librarian. 'The rule is that you must have that card signed by your parents. There's nothing to stop you looking at the books while you're here.'

'All right, then,' said Victor. 'Where do you keep the aeroplanes?'

The librarian thought he was trying to be funny and asked him if he was sure it was a book he wanted.

'We want to look at some books about aircraft,' said Andrew and wondered if Mum was as tiresome as this when she got behind a counter.

'Aircraft are under "Transport",' said the librarian, pointing over her shoulder with a pen.

In Polthorpe Library transport included antique bicycles, skiing and whitewater canoeing. There were only two books on aviation. Victor went back to the desk.

'Could you reserve these for us until Tuesday?' he said.

'I can't reserve books until you are a member,' said the Librarian. 'However, I have to close the library now so no one will want them today. If you come early on Tuesday they'll still be here, won't they? Now put them back tidily.'

Victor replaced the books and followed Andrew to the door. The librarian watched them all the way. When Victor reached the door he turned round,

balled his hand into a fist and stuck out the first and last fingers, like horns, pointing straight at the librarian.

'Don't do that,' said Andrew, hauling him out.

'That's the sign against the evil eye,' said Victor.

11 | Mother and Son

Andrew hoped that Victor would come round and see him on Friday but instead he saw Victor's mother turning in at the gateway. Andrew ran into the kitchen to warn Mum.

'Mrs Skelton's coming up the path,' he said. 'She's coming to see us.'

Mum was leaning over the side of the playpen, handing Edward a piece of bread and butter. He took it in both hands and twisted it in opposite directions like a man tearing up phone directories.

'Coming to see us?' said Mum. 'Or coming to inspect us? Do we get a certificate when she's been?' Mum had heard about Mrs Skelton's housekeeping.

Andrew could hear feet crunching on the gravel at the side of the house. He looked round the kitchen for something to put away and decided to fold up the ironing board. As he propped it against the wall he noticed that Ginger had been walking along it with muddy paws, leaving a trail of pussyfoot prints from one end to the other.

Mrs Skelton was at the back door. Mum was still wrestling with Edward. As she backed away from the playpen he reached up with buttery fingers and grabbed the knot of hair at the back of her neck.

'Buttered bun,' said Andrew. Hairpins dropped out and it unrolled into a long skein with Edward swinging on the end. Mrs Skelton knocked.

Mum rolled up her hair again and drove a skewer through it to keep it in position.

'That's not funny,' said Andrew, seeing the skewer. Mum opened the door and looked down, suddenly. Victor's mother only reached her shoulder.

'Come in, Mrs Skelton,' said Mum. Andrew dodged into the living room, leaving the door open so that he could hear what was going on.

'I'm looking for Victor,' said Mrs Skelton. 'I thought he might have dropped in here.'

'I haven't seen him today,' said Mum. 'Do sit down? Won't you have some coffee?'

There was a thump as Victor's mother sat down.

'I won't stay for coffee, thank you,' she said.

I bet she's afraid of catching something from our cups, thought Andrew.

'Victor seem to come here rather a lot,' said Mrs Skelton. 'I hope he's no trouble to you.'

'No trouble at all,' said Mum. 'No trouble to me, anyway. We like to see him. Besides, he's only been here two or three times.'

'I should think that seem a lot,' said Mrs Skelton. 'It do him good to go about with your Andrew. He don't have many friends. He's a bit backward.'

You old boot, thought Andrew.

'I wouldn't call Victor backward,' said Mum. 'He doesn't seem backward to me. From what Andrew tells me he's very knowledgeable about aircraft. And gorillas. He's very well up on gorillas.'

'What good will that do him?' said Victor's mother, peevishly. 'I think you've got something caught in your hair, at the back, Mrs Mitchell.'

'It's a skewer,' said Mum. She didn't explain why it

was there. Andrew wondered if she was looking embarrassed and doubted it. A chair scraping on the floor told him that Mrs Skelton was getting up to go. Perhaps she was afraid that Mum would whip out the skewer and run amuck. When he heard the door close he went back into the kitchen.

'Eavesdropper,' said Mum. 'What a strange person. She didn't look at me once. She kept staring over my shoulder. What could she have been looking at?'

'The ironing board, I expect,' said Andrew, pointing to the row of footprints along the middle of it.

Mum looked at them admiringly. 'That's neat,' she said. 'That's very neat. You know, we could make a fortune flogging that pattern as trendy wallpaper.'

Someone else knocked at the back door and Andrew went to open it. Victor was standing outside with a slice of bread and butter in his hand.

'I met my Mum in the lane. She told me to give you this,' said Victor. 'What did you give her a bit of bread and butter for?'

'We didn't,' said Mum. 'Oh dear, it's Edward's. He must have put it in her shopping bag while she was sitting by the playpen.'

'Why was she here, then?' asked Victor, stepping into the kitchen so that he could personally return the bread and butter to its owner.

'She said she was looking for you,' said Mum.

'She couldn't have been,' said Victor. 'I was still at home when she went out. I bet she wanted to see what your house is like. She heard me telling my sister what a mess – oh.' Victor stopped, suddenly. 'I didn't say that, exactly.'

'I've never seen your sister,' said Andrew, helpfully. 'I don't believe you've got one.'

'You'll see her picture in the paper, soon enough,' said Victor. 'She's getting married, next month. I wanted her room when she go, but Mum say I'm not to go mucking that up as well. I say, do that skewer go right into your head?'

'No, it doesn't,' said Mum. 'Do you want some coffee?'

'Yes please,' said Victor. He knelt down beside the playpen and poked the bread between the bars. Edward's hand closed on it.

'Feeding time at the zoo,' said Victor. 'Gorillas' tea party. Why don't you put him out in the run with the guinea-pigs?'

'He'd eat them,' said Mum. 'He's a carnivorous baby.'

'That means he eats cars,' said Andrew.

Mum handed round the coffee and they sat on the table to drink it. Victor removed one of his sweaters. It was a warm day.

'I've brought a pile of Mitch Mulligan to cut up,' he said.

'Who is Mitch Mulligan and why are you cutting him up?' asked Mum.

'It's not him we're cutting up, it's the Wellingtons,' said Andrew.

'All is now made clear,' said Mum. 'You've got it in for Mitch Mulligan so you're going to cut up his Wellies. What's he done to deserve it?'

'Bombers, not boots,' said Victor. He went out and brought in the project file and a bundle of *Action*. 'This is Mitch Mulligan, the Wellington Wizard.'

'Thanks very much,' said Mum. 'I'll borrow a couple of these, if I may. I want something to read while Edward finishes his breakfast. What a load of baloney,' they heard her say, as they went upstairs.

'What do she want to read them for?' said Victor.

'She's got to be reading something,' said Andrew. 'Even if it's only the label on the marmalade.'

Victor immediately set to work with the scissors. Andrew sneaked a look at the Marvellous Mystico before he made any cuts.

In half an hour they had cut out several Wellingtons, but none of them was complete. They all had bits missing where the edge of the picture frame cut them off. Victor stuck them on to a piece of paper and Andrew sketched in the parts that were missing. He tried to follow the advice that Mr Coates had given them but it was all too easy to see where the original picture ended and his drawing began.

'Tell you what,' said Victor. 'We ought to trace them. If we get those books out of the library on Tuesday we can trace the photographs. Have you got any toilet paper? The hard kind.'

'We've got some tracing paper, somewhere,' said Andrew. 'I'll go down and look.'

They went downstairs again. Ginger was asleep across the bend in the stairs and they tripped over him. He ran into the kitchen ahead of them, swearing.

'Aha, you feelthy British Pussy Cat,' said Mum as he went by. 'Defiance is useless. Ve haff vays of making you purr.'

'I don't think you'd better read any more of those comics,' said Andrew. 'Where's the tracing paper?'

'How should I know?' said Mum, speaking English again. 'I can't even find the bread knife. There used to be some in the map case, left over from that time you did some tracings for school.'

The map case was a box file containing all the maps that the Mitchells owned. As they had lived in so many places there were plenty of them. The newest were the maps of East Anglia which Dad had bought when they were looking for somewhere to live. They were still muddy from being dropped in the road.

'I can't remember which map I was tracing,' said Andrew, shaking them all to see if anything would fall out. Victor took the map of North East Norfolk and spread it out on the floor.

'I can't read all this little writing,' he complained. 'Where are we?'

'I don't know,' said Andrew. 'I've never looked before. We're quite near the coast, aren't we?'

'About halfway between Polthorpe Broad and the sea. I can see the sea, I can't find the broad. Up here, up here a bit,' muttered Victor, poking with his finger. 'What do that say?'

Andrew leaned over to have a look.

'Trimingham,' he said.

'Wrong Ingham, too far up,' said Victor. 'Here's Polthorpe. That say Polthorpe, don't it?'

'I remember now,' said Andrew. 'I used this map to get across the fields the first day we were here. Our house is on it. Look, here we are. That little dot.'

'Where's my house,' said Victor, still fumbling with the lettering. 'I wonder if I need glasses, I can't read a thing. No, I don't. I just can't read.'

'You could read those tombstones all right,' said Andrew. He thought Victor needed encouraging, especially in view of what his mother had said. Getting him to do the project was a good start.

'If books were as big as tombstones I'd manage O.K.' said Victor. 'What are these little red dots?'

'Our foot path,' said Andrew. 'And here's yours. Look, they meet up at the corner of the churchyard. I didn't know that. Haven't you ever seen a map before?'

'Only in an atlas,' said Victor. 'That didn't look like this. You could get the whole of Norfolk under one hand. Hey, look. There's our school. That's even the right shape. You can see where the canteen stick out at the back.'

He sat back on his heels and surveyed the map from a distance. 'You could have a lot of fun with one of these. That's Norwich, down in the corner. I can read that. What's that spotty looking place just outside it, all done in dots?'

'Norwich Airport. Those dotted lines must be the runways. I wonder if Coltishall's on here. Can you see another place like it?'

'What about this one?'

'That says Rackheath,' said Andrew. 'Is Coltishall near Rackheath?'

'No, miles away. What about this?'

'It can't be there. It's not on the coast. That's Bacton Gas Terminal.'

'Royal Gas Force,' said Victor. 'Is this it?' He pointed to another maze of dotted lines and spelled out 'C-o-l-t. There you are. That's it. Here's the end of the runway and the road going across. This must be where I watch them land. Look at all these little roads going round the edge. Isn't that Firegate Four?'

They examined the area carefully and picked out all the places they had been to.

'Aren't there any more airfields? I thought there would be dozens,' said Andrew.

'There are,' said Victor. 'Get a bigger map.'

'That won't be any good. The bigger the map the smaller the details,' said Andrew. 'It has to be as big as Heathrow or it doesn't show up.' He found the map of North Norfolk, that fitted exactly against the first one. It was patterned all over with the ghostly bones of dead airfields.

'I'd like to visit them all, one day,' said Victor. 'I've been to some already. Marham's a good one. That's not on this map. That's where they have the Victors. You can sit all day and watch them come in. Nothing but Victors, great big things, just like mackerel. Named after me, they are.'

'Get out,' said Andrew. 'What are they really?'

'I told you,' said Victor. 'They're tankers. You know those probes on the Lightnings? They link those up with the fuel lines on the Victors.'

'In the air?'

'Of course,' said Victor. 'If they can refuel in the air they don't have to land so often. How did you think they did it? Come down by a garage and ask for five gallons?'

'I hadn't heard of Victors till you told me,' said Andrew. 'I never even saw a Lightning until we moved here. If we hadn't moved when we did I might never have seen one at all. There won't be any left soon.'

'Yes, there will,' said Victor, sweeping all the maps aside. 'Other countries have Lightnings as well. There'll still be some around, somewhere.'

Andrew wondered why he kept reminding Victor that the Lightnings were going when Victor didn't want to know. He tried to think of a way to apologize.

'Shall we go to Coltishall today?' he said.

'I can't,' said Victor. 'My Mum want me at home this afternoon to dig the garden.'

'What about tomorrow, then?'

'They don't fly on Saturdays,' said Victor. 'Tell you what, we could go on Monday.'

'I can hear something outside now,' said Andrew. 'Quite low.'

'Chipmunk,' said Victor. 'Horrible little things. They're only training planes and they go round and round in circles, for hours. I get properly fed up with them.'

Andrew went to the window and looked up. A small, red and white aircraft with R.A.F. roundels was drooling in circles over the house. He described it to Victor who was still crawling about among the maps.

'Chipmunk. I told you,' said Victor, without looking up. 'I don't want to see that. Bad as a vulture, going round all day. I wouldn't want to see one of them over me if I was dying in the desert.'

Mum came in with Edward under one arm.

'If I put him in the playpen will you keep an eye on him?' she said. 'I want to go round to the Post Office.'

'I'll go round for you,' said Andrew. Edward was peering about, looking for trouble. If he was left with Andrew he would scream and go stiff and purple.

'I'll come with you,' said Victor. Andrew knew what was coming next. 'Can we take Edward in the pram? Can I push him? I'll be ever so careful.'

'You'll go and push him up a telegraph pole, or something,' said Andrew.

'I'll push you up a telegraph pole,' said Victor.

'You'd better fetch the guinea-pigs in before you go,' said Mum. 'It looks to me as if it might rain again.'

'Can't they stay out in the rain?' said Victor. 'Wouldn't they go into their hutch?'

'They haven't got the sense,' said Mum. 'I'm surprised they remember to breathe.'

She put Edward in the pram and fastened him down with a webbing harness. Victor helped Andrew to fetch in the hutch.

'Hello, Kong; hello, Fits,' said Victor, greeting the guinea-pigs through the chicken wire. They were sitting in a friendly heap with Ginger at the end of the pen and whistled angrily when Andrew tried to stuff them into the hutch. Ginger was also put out and ran behind them, making abusive noises.

'I do like Kong,' said Victor as they stowed the hutch under the sink. 'I wish he was mine. Could I sort of be his godfather and borrow him, sometimes?'

'How do you mean, borrow him?' said Andrew. 'Where would you keep him?'

'Not borrow him, exactly,' said Victor. 'Just the idea of him. Then I could tell people I'd got shares in a guinea-pig.'

'Can you really not have one at home?' said Mum. 'You don't have to bring them indoors, most people don't. You could keep it in the shed.'

'No, I couldn't,' said Victor. 'My sister was at school with a girl who caught something off her rabbits and we had to get rid of our budgie.'

'How do you like this, then?' said Mum. 'If you get one you can keep it here. Your mother won't mind that, will she? We'll charge you board and lodging to make it all official and he can live here with ours.'

'Oh,' said Victor, with a grin that showed every last tooth and beyond. 'Oh yes. I know where I can get one. I'll go and ask Mum now. Just a minute.'

'Hang on, what about the Post Office? I'm not going without you,' said Andrew, but Victor had gone.

He came back, a few minutes later, out of breath.

'She say that's all right if I don't kiss it,' he said, looking round the back door. 'I'll get that tomorrow, if that's O.K.?'

They set out for the Post Office. Victor pushed the pram and talked about his imminent guinea-pig.

'I like the way they whistle. The first time I came to your house I thought they were birds in the garden. Can you teach them to whistle tunes? We could get them all to learn the Dambusters' March.'

'How will you do that? You can't whistle yourself,' said Andrew.

'Yes, I can,' said Victor, making a sound like an air raid siren. 'I tried to teach our budgie to whistle. He pulled all his tail feathers out.'

'Why, because of your whistling?' said Andrew. Victor ignored him.

'Look who's coming down the road,' he said.

Riding towards them, very upright on a wiry black bicycle, was the lady from the library. Andrew said 'Good morning,' but she pedalled past them very carefully as if they were an obstruction in the road with red lights round it. Victor scowled as she glided

by and then went into his gorilla routine, behind her back, hopping about, gibbering and scratching. The lady librarian saw him out of the corner of her eye. She slowly stepped off her bicycle and stood quite still, for a full minute, staring at him.

Victor hastily resumed human shape and began chatting to Edward, as though the exhibition had been for his benefit. The librarian got back onto her bicycle and rode away.

They could see what she was thinking, even from behind.

'I don't think we'd better go back to that library,' said Victor.

12 | God Save the Queen

Victor appeared next morning, just after breakfast. Dad was washing up and Mum was reading the paper when he looked round the door, carrying a string bag with a lettuce in it.

'We're here,' said Victor.

'Come in,' said Dad. 'Who's where?'

'Me and my guinea-pig,' said Victor. He put the string bag on the table and folded back the edges of the lettuce. It had been hollowed out and where the heart should have been sat a small, brown guinea-pig, nibbling at the lettuce.

'I thought that'd feel more at home in there,' said Victor.

Ginger jumped onto the table to see what was afoot. He put out a tender paw and patted the guinea-pig in the hope that it would bounce.

'Let's put it in with the others and see how they get on,' said Andrew.

'How do you know they won't fight?' said Dad. 'What sex is yours, Victor? Come to that, what are ours?'

'Male,' said Mum. 'Guinea-boars.'

'Mine's a sow,' said Victor. 'I should have thought of that before. Perhaps we shall get guinea-piglets.'

'I should say that was an absolute dead certainty,' said Dad.

'I wouldn't,' said Mum. 'Ours are very old gents

indeed and Victor's looks far too young to be court-
ing.'

'We shall soon find out,' said Dad. 'Guinea-pigs
being what they are.'

They took the hutch outside and connected it to the
pen. Victor put in the lettuce with the guinea-pig still
inside it. King Kong and Fittipaldi wandered out of
the hutch. King Kong scratched himself. Fittipaldi
went to sleep. Inside the lettuce Victor's guinea-pig
went on with her breakfast.

'I think you ought to change Fittipaldi's name,' said
Victor. 'Who was that fellow who went to sleep for a
hundred years and woke up dead?'

'Rip van Winkle,' said Mum. 'And it was only
twenty years. He was still alive when he woke up.'

'There you are,' said Victor. 'That's what you ought
to call him.'

'What a nerve,' said Andrew. 'How would you like
it if somebody changed your name when you were too
old to look like Victor Skelton?'

'What are you going to call yours?' asked Dad.

'I hadn't thought,' said Victor. 'I could call her
Lightning but that probably won't suit – especially if
she's anything like Fittipaldi. Phantom might be
better. They can go ever so slowly.'

'How about M.R.C.A.?' said Dad.

'What's that?' said Mum. 'Member of the Rodent
Collector's Association?'

'Multi-Role Combat Aircraft,' said Victor. 'No, I
don't think so. That's not a very nice name for a lady
guinea-pig.'

'Queen Kong?' said Andrew.

'Oh, that's good,' said Victor, 'that's what I'll call

her. Did you hear that, Queenie?' he said, into the lettuce.

Andrew was pleased that Victor had chosen his name. He had been afraid that his parents would think of something clever.

Victor would have been happy to stay and look at Queen Kong all morning but his mother wanted him to go shopping in Polthorpe.

'We'll both go,' said Andrew. 'Can I borrow your bike?' he added, quickly, in case Edward was invited to join the party.

'In that case you can get a few things for me,' said Mum, hurrying indoors to make a list.

'I'll keep an eye on Queen Kong for you,' said Dad. Victor bent over the pen.

'Good-bye, Queenie. Good-bye, Kong. Good-bye, Rip van Racing Driver.'

'Look here,' said Andrew. 'He's going to be Fitti-paldi until he dies and then we'll write it on his gravestone.'

They went down the lane to collect the bicycles.

'I'll ask my Mum if you can come over to ours, this afternoon,' said Victor. 'She's going out. We can sit in the lounge and watch the telly.'

'Don't you want to watch your guinea-pig?' said Andrew. He wasn't sure that he wanted to spend the afternoon on Mrs Skelton's shiny black settee that looked as if you would stick to it if you sat there too long.

'Not all the afternoon,' said Victor. 'There's an old war film on, with Lancasters in. I want to watch that. I bet that's the same Lancaster all the way through. That usually is. They've only got the one.'

Polthorpe was a busy place on Saturdays. As well as local people, doing their week-end shopping, there were the visitors from the boats; easily distinguished by their seafaring hats and sweaters thick enough to keep out Atlantic gales. Most of the children were wearing yellow life jackets.

'Watch out,' said Victor, to one boy who shoved past them. 'The tarmac's very deep here. I've seen people drown, just stepping off the pavement.'

The visitors behaved as though the local people were cut out of hardboard and propped up in the street as part of the scenery.

'Townies!' said Victor. 'How would they like it if we went to Birmingham and sat on their window sills and trod on their feet and pushed them in the road.'

Outside the fish and chip shop there was a long queue that stretched back past the church. A lot of people who had bought fish and chips were eating them on the pavement and blocking it. The road was barred by a van unloading timber for the hardware shop.

'Can't get through that lot,' said Victor. 'Let's cut through the churchyard. We can scoot, no one minds. I've seen the vicar do it. He ride a lady's bike.' Victor glided away with one foot trailing, so that no one could accuse him of actually cycling through the churchyard. Andrew followed more cautiously, but the path was smooth with a tempting chicane between the tower and the war memorial. They took the corner rather too quickly and found themselves riding through a wedding. Andrew saw Victor perform a gravity-defying skid and applied his brakes. The bicycle stopped dead and bounced sideways, several times, finally halting beside a big, powdery lady who looked angry enough to be the bride's mother.

A gap opened in the guests and he had a brief glimpse of the vicar and two bridesmaids, in sticky pink satin, skittering about in a blizzard of confetti, and of Victor, making a rapid escape with both feet on the pedals.

Andrew took off after him, trying to apologize without showing his face. They lost themselves in the crowd of chip-eaters round the gate.

'That could have been nasty,' said Victor.'I nearly went straight through the vicar.'

'Did anyone recognize us?' said Andrew.

'I kept my head down,' said Victor. 'But I think we may be in a photograph. A flash bulb went off just as I came round the bridegroom. I'd like to see that photograph. I nearly broke up a funeral in Norwich, once.'

'Not on a bicycle?' said Andrew.

'No, I was walking. There's churches all over the place, in Norwich. You don't see them coming. I was just walking by when this coffin came round the corner, all by itself on a little trolly. That did give me a turn. I nearly fell over it.'

'Was it off to bury itself?' asked Andrew.

'Someone was pushing the trolly,' said Victor. 'But I didn't see him until he came round after it. That did look funny, toddling along, like in a supermarket, but I couldn't laugh, not at a funeral. That's different at a wedding. They all go off and have a drink, afterwards.'

'I expect they all go and have a drink after a funeral,' said Andrew.

'Yes, but that's not right to spoil a funeral,' said Victor. 'After all, that's the last party you ever have.'

'Have you ever been to one, not the one you fell over, I mean,' said Andrew.

'Not yet, but I'm going to a wedding, next month,' said Victor, becoming gloomy. 'I told you. My sister's getting married. She wanted me to wear a suit and carry her train with my cousin Sharon that's going to be bridemaid.'

'You won't, will you?' The thought of Victor, in a suit, mincing up the aisle behind a bride, was too strange to consider seriously.

'Not likely,' said Victor. 'I told her to find some other loony. I said I'd give her away, though. With Green Shield stamps. She hit me.'

'Is your brother going to be there?' asked Andrew, immediately handling the bicycle more carefully.

'Not him,' said Victor. 'He'll be in Hong Kong. Lucky devil.'

'Lucky to be in Hong Kong?'

'No, lucky not to be at my sister's wedding.'

They did the shopping and rode back to Pallingham. When they reached the churchyard Victor said, 'Let's take the short cut.'

'I'd have thought you'd had enough of cutting through churchyards,' said Andrew, but he held the gate open to let Victor through with his shopping bag.

As they walked round the church they heard the sounds of engines in the distance.

'Is that an aircraft?' asked Andrew.

'No, that's on the ground,' said Victor. 'There's that grave I told you about. The one that looks like a bed.'

Under the spread of a dark cedar tree the grave looked just like a fourposter bed with five people tucked snugly into it.

'I wouldn't mind a grave like that,' said Victor. 'Very cosy. Hey, look at that.'

He was gazing over the wall. Andrew joined him. Advancing slowly up the pea field was a row of top-heavy machines, swaying like galleons above the sea of pea plants. The sound of engines, that Andrew had heard, surged ahead of them.

'Pea viners,' said Victor. 'They make a racket. You get lines running up and down the television when they go by. I hope they don't spoil that film this afternoon.'

'What are they doing?' said Andrew. Behind them the field was laid waste, strewn with dead and twisted plants.

'Picking the peas,' said Victor. 'They have to be done all at once when they're ready for freezing. A man come down to look at the crop and if he say that's fit up it come. They won't take them if they're left too long. They have to do that at night, sometimes. I bet that one across from your house will be next.'

'We've got sugar beet opposite us,' said Andrew.

'That don't come up till November,' said Victor. 'I meant the one after that, over by Hemp's farm. You'll hear them, clear enough, if they do that at night.'

The first of the pea viners drew level with them, followed one after the other by the rest of the fleet, spread out in a diagonal line across the field.

Where they had crossed the footpath it survived only as a dotted line, as it was on the map.

'I'm not going to cross that,' said Victor. 'We'll have to go round the long way.'

'Actually,' said Andrew, 'It's quicker if we do,

because we can cycle all the way. It takes another five
minutes to walk across that field.'

'I know that,' said Victor. 'But you can't ask people
to take a long cut, they'd think you were barmy, so
you call that a short cut and they don't know any
better.'

'But why go that way at all, if it's longer?'

'Because I like that,' said Victor. 'And that's as
good a reason as any.'

That night, Andrew was woken by a newly familiar
sound, and the movement of light on the sloping ceiling
above his bed. He went over to the window and looked
out. A procession of lights was moving slowly along the
hedge at the end of the beet field and he remembered
seeing something like it before. Once, when he was very
small, he had stood with his father, beside a river, in the
dark, and had seen the riding lights of ships moving
soundlessly past them in the night.

Now he saw the same sight again but attended by
the distant drubbing of engines. He supposed that the
ships had had engines too but all he could recall was
the silent movement over the water: in fact, he wasn't
sure that he could recall it at all. Perhaps he could
only remember remembering.

What he saw now were the pea viners riding out to
clear the field next to Hemp's Farm, as Victor had
forecast.

He stood for a long time in the chilly patch of air by
the window until the shuddering line of lights had
turned the corner by the straw stack and disappeared
behind the hedge. Then he went back to bed.

In the morning, the field was empty.

13 | Unknown Warrior

'It always rains when we go to Coltishall,' said Andrew, on Monday morning.

'Not really surprising,' said Mum. 'You've only been once and it's rained every other day since we came here.'

'It's raining today and we're going today,' said Andrew. He went to the front door to see if there was a break in the clouds. On the doorstep were fat brown slugs, like hovercraft, with frilly orange skirts, taking advantage of the wet weather to travel by daylight. Ginger sprinted across the road, trying to keep all four feet off the ground at once and trilling his leg irritably when he stepped in a puddle.

He came up onto the step and interfered with the slugs which immediately became very small, reminding Andrew of a certain type of cough lozenge, half sucked. He picked them up and put them into the iris leaves by the front door, where no one could step on them. Ginger, his fur soaked into cactus spines, pushed past him and ran into the living room. Andrew went out into the rain to search for the prevailing wind. Close to the house it came from all directions at once like a mean child who jeered round corners and disappeared when you followed it.

Out on the road there was no doubt that the wind was in the south, carrying with it a streak of blue sky. A wind that brought fine weather to Pallingham would bring it also to Coltishall. He went back indoors, for breakfast.

Edward had been promoted to a highchair and sat in it now, exploring the back of his mouth with one hand and mashing up a rusk with the other. Andrew took his toast to a place of safety on the other side of the table, and settled down to eat. No doubt Victor was also eating his breakfast at this very moment, sitting down to a clean table-cloth, properly laid, in his cold kitchen. Most of Andrew's kitchen table was taken up with record catalogues and gramophone reviews.

Mum and Dad had come by twenty pounds, unexpectedly, and were now discussing what records to buy with it. Dad was making a list to take into Norwich with him. Andrew knew that they would spend the evening listening to the records, and discussing them. He wondered, if, by some happy chance, Victor would invite him over to his house, so that he wouldn't have to listen.

'Is there anything you fancy out of our ill-gotten gains?' said Mum, aiming spoonsful of egg towards Edward.

'What are they?' asked Andrew.

'Our money,' said Mum. 'Not really ill-gotten. It was my old Post Office Savings book. It turned up while we were unpacking.'

Andrew had a Savings book. It contained ninety five pence. 'Do I have to have records?' he said.

'Of course not, you tone-deaf monster,' said Dad. 'Anything you like, within reason.'

'Could I have a book on aircraft?' he said. 'If it didn't cost too much.'

'Military aircraft?' said Dad. 'There are plenty of those about. Or did you want something that deals with everything from Sopwith-Camel to Concorde?'

'It had better have Lightnings in it,' said Andrew.

'I'll see what I can do,' said Dad. He went out by the back door. The sad sound of rain filled the room before he could close it behind him.

'You won't go out if it's like this, will you?' said Mum. 'Oh Edward, get that into your mouth, do, you noisome baby.'

'It looked like it was going to clear up,' said Andrew. 'Have you fed the guinea-pigs?'

The three of them were gathered hopefully in the hutch, looking up at Ginger who was sitting wetly on the wire netting. King Kong and Fittipaldi seemed scarcely to have noticed that they had company. Queen Kong minded her own business and still slept in the lettuce. Andrew lifted Ginger onto the floor and put a bowl of food into the hutch. The three animals converged on it and Ginger tried to climb in as well, assuming that any bowl of food was meant for him.

'Give him some milk,' said Mum. 'Is Victor coming here or are you calling for him?'

'He's coming here,' said Andrew. 'Honestly, I think you need a passport to get into his house when his Mum's there. I can hear him coming now.'

Footsteps sounded on the gravel and Victor came to the back door draped in a ground sheet to protect the raincoat that he wore over his anorak. He carried a bunch of carrot tops.

'Hello, Mrs Mitchell; hello, Edward; hello, pigs,' said Victor. 'Do they eat carrot tops?' he asked, pushing the greenery through the wire. Ginger rushed back to the hutch, took a carrot top and pulled it out again with dainty teeth.

'Unnatural animal,' said Mum. 'He can't bear to miss anything. Last night he was licking pickle off the plates after dinner.'

'Are you fit?' asked Victor. 'The weather forecast say sunny periods coming up.' To prove his faith in the forecast he hung his ground sheet over a chair and removed his raincoat as well. Andrew gathered that he was beginning to feel at home.

Victor had left the bicycles against the coalshed door, out of the rain. As he and Andrew came out of the house a cold, damp wind slid over the guttering and caught them across the back of the neck, like a guillotine. Victor frisked his bicycle for rust spots before wheeling it out of its shelter, but already the rain drops were falling farther apart and the clouds were pulling away to the coast, leaving a lagoon of clear sky in the south west. In the middle of it shone a bright yellow spot, a lesser sun.

'Air-Sea Rescue,' said Victor. The yellow dot was a helicopter, whirling seawards. 'Here that come, choppa-choppa-choppa-choppa. I wonder if that's going to rescue someone or only out on practice.'

The helicopter clattered over on its way to the sea.

As they were approaching the airfield it passed them on its return journey. They watched it sink from sight below the trees. After the thud of its rotors had stopped they heard the whine of the generator that started the Lightnings.

'Full speed to the firegate,' cried Victor, accelerating.

As they raced up the lane to the firegate they heard

the roar of engines and a Lightning went by on the runway, rising into the air at the very moment it drew level with the gate.

Victor and his bicycle parted company. The bicycle dropped into the grass by the fence and Victor flung himself at the gate, craning over it to watch the aircraft climb. By the time Andrew had dismounted it was almost out of sight, a glassy speck in the sunshine.

'I suppose it was using its re-heats,' said Andrew. 'If I'd known I'd have got off a bit faster.'

'The one we heard start up, that's going to take off in a minute,' said Victor. 'That's at the end of the runway now.'

Andrew took his place beside Victor, on the gate.

'You haven't seen one take off from here yet, have you?' said Victor. 'You'd better cover your ears.'

'I've seen them land. It's not so bad,' said Andrew.

'That's a bit different when they go up,' said Victor. 'You'll see. Here she come.'

The crouching, growling, grey beast at the end of the runway sprang forwards. It moved too quickly to follow with the eye. Before Andrew had really noticed it was moving it was off the ground. The noise was so enormous he felt as if he was being sucked through the jets himself. He clapped his hands over his ears, lost his balance and fell off the gate.

'Blown over, eh?' said Victor, sparing him a hasty glance while following the upward path of the Lightning. Andrew picked himself up.

'It's all right for you, you're used to it,' he said. 'I bet you've forgotten what it was like the first time.'

'You ought to do what I say,' said Victor. 'I told you to cover your ears. You never believe me,' he added, smug in the knowledge that his own large ears were equal to the noise.

After the last rumble of the engines had died away the empty air still trembled above the runway. The grounded Lightnings stood in a quiet row and there was no sign of the mechanics who had crawled over them before. The helicopter stood on its pad with drooping rotors, looking like a dog that has been severely scolded. Victor leaned on the gate and looked worried.

'You know, every time I come here there's less and less going on. I'm sure they don't fly as much as they used to. This time last year there were Lightnings going up and down all the time. They even had an aerobatic team of Lightnings at the Open Day.'

'Perhaps they're falling to bits,' said Andrew. 'They look old enough. If they're not going to be used any more there's no point in repairing them.'

'That's not so simple,' said Victor.'They can't just let them fall apart. They have to be maintained right up to the very last time they're used.'

'There's a Lightning moving now,' said Andrew, seeing a tail fin glide behind the standing aircraft.

'I can't hear anything,' said Victor, and as the moving aircraft came out from behind the others they saw that it was being towed. It turned very slowly, showing mute exhausts, and disappeared into the hangar.

'Perhaps they aren't being maintained any more and that's why they're not flying,' said Andrew and then realized that it wasn't the kindest thing he could have said.

They waited for half an hour but no more Lightnings went up and the two that had taken off earlier did not return. The only thing that moved was the helicopter. It rose from its pad, crossed the runway and hung about near the trees, neither landing nor flying; dithering in the air.

Andrew thought that even one take-off was worth seeing, but Victor became restless.

'I don't like it when they're not flying,' he said. 'Let's go away for a bit. That should bring something. I bet if we went home they'd all take off.' He picked his bicycle out of the fence where it had become entangled when he threw it down. 'We'll go round to the end of the runway and see if anything come.'

While they were on their way the two Lightnings returned and circled the airfield prior to landing. In spite of riding as dangerously fast as they could the aircraft had touched down before they had arrived at the gap in the hedge. There was only the smell of burned oil to show that they had ever been there. The sky, now quite clear of cloud, held nothing but a Chipmunk grinding endless circles overhead.

'I've never known that so bad,' said Victor, glaring into the empty sky above the rows of lights as though by staring he could make something appear. Andrew wandered up and down the side of the cabbage field, picking unripe blackberries out of the hedge. He knew that Victor was uneasy because he was afraid that soon the Lightnings would never fly again. Or because the two that had just landed might have been the last and Victor hadn't known. He also knew that his own remarks had been tactless, to say the least. Andrew could think of nothing that he could say to please him. He wished it was possible to divert him with talk of racing cars or the Land Speed Record.

On the other side of the road was a low building with a red light on the roof. He had noticed it on the previous visit but there had been no chance to ask about it.

'What's that little house over there?' he asked. 'Why is there a light on the roof?'

Victor looked, without interest.

'That's got a light on because that's near the runway. I don't know what that is, though. I never bothered to look, before. There was always so much else to look at. That little bit of ground round it is a sort of cemetery.'

'It's a funny place to have a cemetery,' said Andrew. 'What's it like? I'm going over to have a look.'

'That's only old graves,' said Victor.

'I thought you liked old graves.'

'Not when I'm here,' said Victor, but he left the gap in the hedge and crossed the road with Andrew.

The cemetery lay behind a thorn hedge and a tall iron gate. Between the road and the little building the graves lay warmly in the sunlight, bedded in tidy grass. It seemed a nice place to be buried in, if you had to be buried at all. He forgot that it was almost on the runway.

They went up to the building. Its wooden doors were locked firmly against them. Andrew walked round to the side where there was a window with little diamond panes. He put his face close to the dusty glass and looked in. All he could see was the window opposite, old chairs and a curious vehicle that looked like a wide wooden ladder with high wheels, one each side of it.

Victor looked over his shoulder.

'That's a bier. That's what they put the coffins on.'

'Like the one you met in Norwich?'

'No, that was a little tinny thing. This is like the one they've got at Pallingham. You could do all sorts of things with that,' said Victor. 'If you got the two of them together you could have bier races.'

'This looks like a fancy sort of shed to keep a bier in,' said Andrew.

'I think that's a chapel,' said Victor. 'Perhaps when they have a funeral they take that out. That don't look like they've had a funeral for years, do it?'

Behind the chapel the cemetery stretched away into the fields, shadowed by its high hedges. On one side were more old graves, well settled into the earth. On the other side the headstones were white and upright, all the same; rank upon rank stood to attention in front of a tall cross on a stepped plinth.

'Those are war graves,' said Victor.

The stones were arranged in rows of five. Andrew and Victor went to examine them more closely. All were marked with the R.A.F. insignia, carved into the stone, the name of a man and the dates of his birth and death.

'Did they die in the Battle of Britain?' said Andrew.

'Some of them maybe,' said Victor, tracing a name with his finger. 'Not most of them, though. A lot of these dates are much later.'

'They aren't all English,' said Andrew. 'This one came from Canada and flew with the R.A.F.' He moved to another row. 'This one was in the Australian Air Force.'

'Look at these,' said Victor, up ahead. 'These are

properly foreign. I can't read the names at all.' He was standing by a row of stones a little different from the others. Instead of bearing the encircled wings of the R.A.F. they were carved with small crosses. Andrew bent to look at the names.

'I think they're German,' he said.

'Germans?' said Victor. 'Buried here? The enemy?'

'They couldn't not bury them, could they?' said Andrew. 'They must have been shot down over here in a battle. Once they were dead they weren't the enemy any more. If they were alive now, they wouldn't be the enemy any more, would they?'

'Just think,' said Victor. 'This chap here,' he pointed to one of the English graves, 'might have been killed by that chap there. And now they're buried beside each other.'

'Not quite,' said Andrew. 'The Germans are in a row on their own. There are three more over there, but they haven't put anyone else beside them to finish the row.'

'Perhaps they didn't think that would be right,' said Victor. He paused by the middle stone of the row. 'What do this one say? That's not quite the same as the others.'

Andrew looked. On the middle stone it said only: *Ein Deutscher Soldat.*

'They didn't know his name,' said Andrew. 'I think it means, a German soldier. No one ever knew who he was.'

'Perhaps the others were his mates,' said Victor. 'I don't suppose anybody ever knew what happened to him; his family, or anyone. He just didn't come home.

And we know he's here, but we don't know who he was.'

'Steve Stone ought to be here somewhere,' said Andrew.

'Steve Stone? Him in the comic? What's he got to do with it?'

'Nothing,' said Andrew. 'That's the point. Steve Stone and Mitch Mulligan, they're all explosions and crashes and people getting blown up, but you never see anybody dead. There are never any pictures like this. *Ein Deutscher Soldat.* In all those stories he's just the Hun and serve him right.'

'Perhaps they don't want people to think what really happened,' said Victor. 'War's supposed to be fun.'

'It's only fun in comics,' said Andrew. 'But in real life it hurts just as much whichever side you die on. And you're just as dead afterwards.'

'Let's go back to the road,' said Victor. 'I don't like that, here. It's sad.'

They returned to the gap in the hedge and waited again, but the Lightnings stayed in their sullen rows by the hangars. The only movement was the tireless turning of the Radar scanners. Even the Chipmunk had gone.

'Shall we go home?' said Andrew. 'It doesn't look as though anything else is going to happen.'

'Let's just wait a bit longer,' said Victor. 'Something might come.' But nothing did.

14 | Education

Dad came home that evening with a thick parcel of records under one arm.

'I caught the August end of the July sales,' he said. 'I've got all we wanted and a few more. I've got something for you, too,' he said, as he saw Andrew eyeing his briefcase. He took out two books. 'This one is about aircraft in the Second World War. The other is a bit more up to date. I had a look through it in the shop. I think I saw everything that's ever flown over this house.'

Andrew took the books upstairs to look at them. His room was so covered in bits of paper that there was nowhere to sit. He cleared a space among the racing cars and sat on the shelf. From downstairs he heard the sound of music. Mum and Dad were playing one of their new records. In his cot, Edward would be lying back, enjoying it. He liked music, even Mum's singing. Andrew gathered up all the pieces of paper, put them in the project file and went down again. As he went into the living room each of his parents held up a warning hand in case he interrupted the record. It sounded like bawling and squeaking and twanging bedsprings to him.

'Can I take the books down to show Victor?' he asked, when the noise died down.

'Do you think they'll let you in?' said Mum.

'I'll clean my shoes before I go,' said Andrew and he went to do it.

When he knocked on Victor's door it was opened by a young woman he had never met before. She looked like Victor, only bigger in all directions.

'Are you Cheryl?' asked Andrew, holding the books before him as a shield.

'Victor's in his room,' said Cheryl, although she hadn't admitted that that was who she was. 'You'd better go up.'

Andrew stepped inside, wiping his feet loudly. In order to get to the stairs he had to pass through the lounge, where Mr and Mrs Skelton were watching television. Worse still, he had to walk between them and the television set. Victor's mother nodded as he went by. His father made a threatening movement with his head. Andrew closed the door behind him and crept upstairs. Outside Victor's room he stopped and knocked.

Victor opened the door cautiously as though he expected hoodlums on the landing. When he saw that it was Andrew he opened the door properly and beckoned him in. Although it was still light, Victor had drawn the curtains and switched on his fifteen watt bulb. The aircraft hung among fantasy shadows, turning gently in the breeze from the open window. Andrew bent double and followed Victor across the room to the bed. On the pillow stood a model Lightning, detached from its string. Judging by the long dent down the middle of the bedspread Victor had been lying there, looking at it.

'My Dad bought me some aircraft books. I've got them here,' said Andrew. 'Can we have a bit more light?'

'I've got another bulb, somewhere,' said Victor. 'I

put that in when my Mum say I'm ruining my eyesight. I take that out again when she's forgotten.'

He dug a spare bulb out of the chest of drawers and screwed it into the socket. To do this he had to climb onto the bed. As he stood down again there was a sharp crunch from among the bedclothes. He pulled out a plastic Hurricane with one wing broken off.

'That must have come down while I was out. I didn't notice. Wizard prang,' he said, dropping it on the floor. Andrew picked it up again.

'Can't you stick it together?'

'I'll hang that up by the tail and pretend that's coming down in flames,' said Victor.

Andrew put the Hurricane on the window sill and laid the broken wing beside it.

'I've got the folder here, as well,' he said. 'And some tracing paper. These books are full of photographs and diagrams. There's a whole lot about Lightnings in this one.'

Victor sat down on the bed and took the book.

'You know what?' he said. 'When the Jaguars come I bet they scrap all the Lightnings. People will forget what great planes they were and they'll all be broken up.'

'But you said there were lots of them in other countries,' said Andrew. 'They might be around for years yet.'

'They won't be here,' said Victor. 'I shan't see them. That's just like the end of the war. When the fighting planes were finished with, they scrapped them, because they weren't needed any more. That wasn't till afterwards they realized there weren't any left and they had to go round looking for bits to put together again.'

'Perhaps when the war was ended they just wanted to forget about it. They like remembering now, because we won and anyway, it's been over for years. I bet people wouldn't be so keen on that old Lancaster if it wasn't the only one left,' said Andrew.

'Lightnings never won any wars,' said Victor. 'There won't be anything to remember them for. When I'm grown up and I tell people that I can remember when Lightnings flew over every day, no one will care. They won't know what I'm talking about.'

'They might not all be scrapped,' said Andrew. 'You might be wrong.'

'I might be,' said Victor. 'Where have all the Hawker Hunters gone?' he shouted. Andrew blinked. 'I don't know. Where have they gone?'

'I don't know either,' said Victor. 'But there don't seem to be any left. Not long ago there were still a couple flying about round here. I haven't seen them in months.'

'Well, then,' said Andrew. 'Let's get on with our project. It'll be something to remind you when they have gone.'

'I don't need reminding,' said Victor. 'That's all in here.' He pointed to his head.

Andrew opened the book at the page about Lightnings, placed a sheet of tracing paper in it and handed it to Victor who balanced the book unsteadily on his knees and began to draw round the photograph.

Andrew opened the other book.

'Shall I do a Lancaster? We haven't got one of those yet.'

Victor didn't answer. He was muttering his way

round the nose cone. The Lancaster had a very simple outline. Andrew had finished his tracing long before Victor had reached the tailplane. His Lightning had been photographed with a full weapon load and it was lumpy with missiles. He gave up before he had worked his way round to the refuelling probe.

'That's no good,' he said. 'I can't even trace properly. I wish somebody would invent a machine so that you could just think pictures onto paper. I've got a lovely idea in my head, at the end of the runway where the lights are. There's one Lightning coming in and another one levelling out, behind it. It comes screaming down–' he dived with his hand, to illustrate. 'I can see it all, even with my eyes open, but I can't get that down. I'd better do something else.'

'Can you make notes about the Lancaster?' said Andrew. 'To go with my tracing. I'll read them out and you copy them down.'

This took a long time. Victor wrote very slowly, going back over the letters to make sure that they stayed put. Andrew watched him.

'Wouldn't it be worth learning to write properly so that you could put down all you know about Lightnings?'

'Why should I put that all down?' said Victor. 'I know that already. I'm only writing this lot for the project. I don't need to.' He meant, I'm only doing it because you say so.

'Don't let's do it then,' said Andrew. 'Don't let's do a project at all. You were right. As soon as you put it on paper it stops being interesting.'

'I know I was right,' said Victor. 'Look at you and your racing cars. You never thought about doing a project on them until old Miss Beale suggested it. I bet you haven't even looked at that since the end of term.'

'I've been too busy chasing aeroplanes, said Andrew. 'I've hardly looked at a car since I took up with you.'

Victor was putting all the papers away.

'If we're not going to do a project,' he said, 'Let's just look at the pictures. I'd enjoy that. You can read out the bits underneath and I'll tell you what they mean.'

'No,' said Andrew. '*You* read out the bits underneath and I'll tell you if you've got them right.'

Victor looked at him, hard.

'That's no good, you know,' he said. 'That's no good you trying to teach me anything. I'll never be any use. I don't think I even want to be. If you start being good at something, people expect you to be even better and then they get annoyed when you aren't. That's safer to seem a bit dafter than you are.'

'But you're not daft,' said Andrew. 'I thought you were at first, till I knew you better. The same as the first time I saw you I thought you were fat. I didn't know you were dressed in layers. Why do you wear so many clothes? Don't you get hot?'

'Now and again,' said Victor, 'but I don't care. I like wearing all my clothes at once. I felt all wrong on Prize Day, just wearing a shirt and trousers. I felt like I'd come out in my skin. I might just as well have worn everything, no one would have noticed. I didn't get a prize. I could have come in a hearth rug. You don't catch me up on the platform winning a book I don't want to read.'

'But don't you care if people think you're stupid?'

'No, I don't,' said Victor. 'Why be miserable just to make other people happy?'

Andrew went home at nine o'clock, leaving the books behind for Victor to look at. As he left the house he noticed that the light was shining brightly behind the bedroom curtains, but when he looked back, a few moments later, he saw that it had become dim again and he knew that Victor was stretched out on his bed, under the bomber's moon, watching the aeroplanes as they turned silently against the ceiling.

15 | Clean Sheet

'Someone has put a cryptic message through the letter box,' said Mum. 'And it's got your name on it. It looks like a blackmail threat in code. Have you been consorting with known criminals?' She handed it to Andrew. It was written on a piece of his own tracing paper and said, 'lets. go. t. chlotsal Trusdy.'

'It's from Victor,' said Andrew. 'He wants to go to Coltishall on Thursday.'

'Today is Thursday,' said Mum. 'Perhaps he means Friday.'

'I don't think even Victor would spell Friday like that,' said Andrew. 'He might mean Tuesday or he might have thought today was Wednesday. He must have been in a hurry, there are no question marks. I'll go down and ask him in a minute.'

'We haven't seen much of him this week,' said Mum. 'I thought he'd be in and out all the time, looking at his guinea-pig. Maybe he doesn't care about it so much now that he's got it.'

'He was here yesterday, while you were taking Edward to the clinic,' said Andrew. 'He's a bit fed up at the moment, because of the Lightnings going. I wish I hadn't told him. I should have waited till he told me.'

'I should have thought that Victor would be all in favour of progress, especially in the field of avionics,' said Mum.

'Well, he's not,' said Andrew, thinking that Mum had no business using words like avionics. 'It's just that the Lightnings have been here since he was little. He's not used to changes, not like we are. He'll feel a bit lost when they've gone, I think. When we went to Coltishall on Monday there was hardly anything going on. I thought he was going to cry.'

'He wouldn't though, would he?' said Mum. 'Victor doesn't like people to see him as he really is. I suppose that's why he makes himself look so out-rageous, to put us off the scent. I wonder, perhaps that's why you and he get on so well; you are just the opposite.'

'What do you mean?' said Andrew, on guard. He usually tried to avoid serious conversations with Mum. She was too old to feel ashamed of herself afterwards.

'Well, anyone can see what you're thinking,' said Mum.

'No they can't,' said Andrew. 'You couldn't see that I was afraid of going to school.'

'Oh yes, I could,' said Mum. 'That's why I made you start at once, instead of next term. You'd have been dead of fright by September. Now you know what to expect and you've got a friend to go back with.'

'Why didn't you say something then?' asked Andrew.

'I did,' said Mum. 'I said, "The first day's always the worst" and you thought it was a big con. If I'd tried to talk you round, you wouldn't have taken any notice. You were determined to hate it long before you got there.'

'I did hate it at first,' said Andrew. 'It was an absolute muddle to begin with.'

'I know,' said Mum. 'One look at your sulky mug as you came up the path on the first day and I could tell exactly what you thought. But the muddle's over now, isn't it? You know who you'll get on with, and which teachers are idiots and who you wouldn't touch with a bargepole.'

'Jeannette Butler,' said Andrew, at once. 'I wouldn't touch her with a pick axe. She's just like a scaly dinosaur. Victor said, "Give us a kiss," and she poked him.'

'You wait till Victor's a bit older,' said Mum, 'and he won't have to ask. She'll give at the knees when he goes by.'

'With his teeth?' said Andrew.

'She won't be looking at his teeth,' said Mum. Andrew thought the conversation was becoming rather silly.

'I expect we shall go to Coltishall this afternoon,' he said. 'I'll nip down to Victor's now and make sure.'

Victor was out when he got there. His mother answered the door and kept a squeegee mop between him and the kitchen floor, which was being cleaned again.

'I'll give him your message,' she said. 'He's gone to Polthorpe with the washing. The machine's broken down.'

'Do you want my father to look at it?' said Andrew. 'He's good with electrical things. He works on a computer.'

'It was a computer that sent us an electricity bill for ninety two pounds,' said Victor's mother, closing the door.

Andrew went back up the lane and met Victor

cycling home with a plastic bag full of washing, jammed between the handlebars.

'Why did you put a note through the door?' asked Andrew. 'You should have come in.'

'I was in a hurry to get to the launderette,' said Victor, sitting at ease with his chin resting on the bag of washing. 'If you don't get there before half past nine that's full of ladies with babies crawling about.'

'I'd have thought you'd like it full of babies,' said Andrew. 'You can take Edward along with you next time, if you like.'

'That's not safe,' said Victor. 'They crawl all over everything. I'm always afraid that one of them will get churdled up in the tumble drier. Are you coming, this afternoon?'

'I've just been down to tell you that,' said Andrew. 'Your Mum's cleaning the floor again. Do you want to come in and have a coffee while it dries?'

'O.K.,' said Victor, turning the bicycle round. 'There's always coffee going at your house, isn't there? Do your Mum keep that pot boiling all day?'

'It's not a pot, it's a percolator,' said Andrew. 'I wish she'd buy instant coffee. She fills it up in the morning and just keeps adding water all day. When it comes out grey it's time for a new lot.'

'We have coffee at eleven in the morning and half past three in the afternoon,' said Victor. 'Never in between. I wouldn't care how grey that was if I could just have that when I wanted it.'

When they reached Andrew's house he left Victor greeting the guinea-pigs and went in to light the gas under the percolator. Mum was at the table, slapping a foggy piece of pastry onto the top of a pie dish.

'Shepherd's pie,' she said. 'Plenty of vegetables, but not very much shepherd. There was less meat on that bone than I thought.'

'You don't make shepherd's pie with pastry,' said Andrew.

'We're almost out of potatoes too,' said Mum.

'I'll get you some from the Post Office,' said Andrew. 'If you let me buy some instant coffee as well.'

'You should count yourself lucky to get real coffee,' said Mum, tweaking at the pastry to make it fit.

'The happiest moment of my life,' said Andrew, looking at the ceiling, 'was the day we moved out and you packed the percolator at the bottom of the crockery box.' Mum threw the pastry brush at him.

Ginger sneaked round the mixing bowl to help remove the pastry trimmings from the pie. Mum hauled him off.

'You watch out, lad, or you'll be in the pie as well. There's plenty of meat on him,' she said, putting him on the floor. 'We'll fatten him up for Christmas.'

'Don't you go cooking our guinea-pigs,' said Victor, at the door.

'Now, there's an idea,' said Mum. 'Guinea-pig pasties: fricasée of guinea-pig: guinea-pig au gratin: whole roast guinea-pig with an apple in its mouth.'

'A pea,' said Andrew.

'I couldn't eat anything I'd looked after,' said Victor. 'Rabbits or chickens and that. My uncle bought twelve cockerels and reared them to eat, but when that came to killing them he had to take them down the road to Charlie Hemp. He didn't mind eating them, though, once their heads were off. He didn't like the way they looked at him after they were dead.'

'Coffee's perking,' said Andrew. 'Have we got any clean cups?'

'I haven't washed up yet,' said Mum. 'Just run them under the tap.' She jabbed three holes in the top of the pie crust and put the dish in the oven. A nasty smell floated out when she opened the door.

'It's the remains of that chicken we had at the weekend,' said Andrew. 'They've been cooking while the oven heated up.'

'They've been burning,' said Mum, taking a dish of black bones out of the oven. 'Put them somewhere to cool, will you? If I put them in the dustbin now, they'll burn a hole in it'

Andrew put down the cups and carried the smoking dish into the garden. Ginger followed him and offered to take the chicken off his hands.

'Chicken bones are bad for cats,' said Andrew. 'They'll stick in your throat.' But Ginger ignored him and dragged the carcase away by one leg. Andrew watched him trying to kill it in the flower bed and went back indoors. Victor was serving coffee. He gave Andrew Edward's mug with the rabbits on. Mum took the cup with only half a handle and propped herself against the fridge.

'How's Mutt Michigan getting along?' she asked Victor. 'Still winning the war single-handed, armed only with his Stilson wrench?'

'Mitch Mulligan,' said Victor. 'And that's a spanner, not a wrench. I don't know. I didn't get that this week.'

'What? Aren't you going to find out if he gets back inside the aircraft?' said Andrew.

'Of course he get back inside,' said Victor. 'That's the trouble. You know nothing will ever happen to him. By rights, he should have had his head blown off by now, but he still go on, week after week. I'm going off him,' he added.

'Well, if that's so,' said Mum, 'I'll let you in on a secret. When I was at school my young brother used to have a comic and Mitch Mulligan was in it, only he wasn't called Mitch Mulligan then. He was Block Buster the Wellington Wonder, but the pictures were the same and by the looks of it, so were the stories. I recognized him at once.'

'Did you read them, then?' asked Victor.

'Oh yes,' said Mum. 'I used to enjoy them, too. They were much more exciting than the girls' comics. Those were all about how Trudy unmasked the Phantom Hoaxer and saved the school from ruin; or how Sally Stringbag danced her way to fame with a wooden leg and saved her father from ruin. I expect they still are,' she said.

When Victor had stopped giggling, he said, 'I'd better get those sheets back home. I'll be skinned, else. Shall I see you after lunch, then?'

'I'll come down with you, if you like,' said Andrew. 'I'm going to get some coffee.'

'Spuds,' said Mum.

'Coffee and spuds,' said Andrew.

'Fair enough,' said Mum. 'Care to take Edward with you? Of course you would.'

Edward was shadow boxing in his pram by the front door.

'Hello, gorillakins,' said Victor. 'Don't knock your-self out.'

Edward smiled at him and put his foot in his mouth.

'I wish I could do that,' said Victor. 'I used to be able to. When I was little I bit my nails. When I ran out of fingers I used to bite my toenails.'

'You still do bite your nails,' said Andrew, looking at Victor's nibbled fingertips.

'But not my toenails,' said Victor. 'I can't reach any more; I'm getting old and stiff.'

Andrew put the bag of sheets on the end of the pram and walked down the lane. At Victor's house he left the pram at the gate and carried the bag round to the back door while Victor put his bicycle away. He held the bag round the middle. The folded top blossomed open and released a soothing smell of clean washing.

Victor opened the door and took the bag from him. The top sheet was squeezed out of the bag and fell onto the path. Victor sidestepped in a desperate rescue bid and put his foot on it. When Andrew picked up the sheet he saw that one side was freckled with mossy green spots while the other was heavily imprinted with the sole of Victor's boot. He looked up and saw Victor's mother standing in the doorway.

She looked at him, at Victor and at the sheet, then without saying anything, she smacked Victor hard, three times, across the side of the head. Victor rocked on his feet and put his hand to his head, but he said nothing either.

Andrew was shocked by the silence of it. In his house, any trouble was accompanied by much shouting and table-thumping, all over in a few moments because no one could ever get angry enough to keep it up. He gaped at Mrs Skelton.

'It was my fault,' he said. 'I let the bag open.'

Mrs Skelton didn't look at him. She flicked the back of her hand towards Victor's face.

'Take that back this afternoon,' she said to him.

'We were going out this afternoon. Can't we take it now?' said Andrew. 'I'll take it. My mother will wash it if you like.'

'This afternoon,' said Mrs Skelton, and took the bag of washing into the kitchen.

Andrew gave Victor the soiled sheet. 'I'll see you when you get back. We can go out afterwards,' he said, but Victor only shook his head and followed his mother indoors.

'She hit him,' said Andrew. 'Only for dropping the sheet; and it wasn't his fault at all, it was mine. It just came out of the bag by itself but it was me that let the bag come open.'

'I dare say she knew that,' said Mum. 'It was probably you she wanted to hit and she took it out on Victor instead. Some people have to lash out when they're angry. I do. I kick the furniture.'

'Yes, and you only hurt your toe,' said Andrew. 'She wanted to hurt him, I could see. And the sheet wasn't all that dirty. I've seen you put dirtier sheets back on the bed.'

'I didn't say she was right,' said Mum. 'I was trying to explain.'

'It wasn't fair.'

'Nothing's fair,' said Mum. 'There's no such thing as fairness. It's a word made up to keep children quiet.

When you discover it's a fraud then you're starting to grow up. The difference between you and Victor is that you're still finding out and he knows perfectly well already. He doesn't even think it worth mentioning. I bet you've never heard him say, "It's not fair," have you?'

'I suppose not,' said Andrew. 'But she shouldn't have hit him. I don't care whether he expects it or not, that doesn't make it right.'

'What price a clean house?' said Mum.

'I don't believe that's got anything to do with it,' said Andrew."Some people are just nasty.'

16 | Takeover

Andrew looked out of his window on Friday morning and saw Victor in a fisherman's smock and foootball jersey toiling up the lane with the two bicycles. Andrew whistled and Victor looked up. Having both hands full he couldn't wave, but he grinned. Andrew observed that the grin was as wide as ever: quite undented. He ran downstairs.

'It looks as though we're going out this morning,' he said, as he passed Mum on the landing. 'Victor's got both the bikes again.'

'I hope you have better luck today,' said Mum.

'So do I,' said Andrew. Thursday afternoon, when they should have been at Coltishall, had been loud with aircraft. He had spent most of the afternoon in the garden watching a tantalizing succession of planes wheeling against a sky already grazed by vapour trails. He felt guilty because he was watching and Victor was exiled in the launderette with the sheet.

When he went round to the gate Victor was already in the garden, exchanging silly noises with Edward.

'When he get a bit bigger we can take him with us,' he said. 'Train him up right. My auntie's got a seat on the back of her bike to put a baby on. We'll borrow that for Edward.'

'I don't think he'd like the noise,' said Andrew, with an awful vision of himself in the years ahead, carting Edward about on the back of a bicycle.

'Next year, maybe,' said Victor. 'Let's get going. I don't want to waste any more time today.'

Mum came out of the front door with a vacuum flask. She held it up like Florence Nightingale and then tucked it into Victor's saddle bag.

'The coffee was hot, so I put some in here,' she said. 'Andrew told me you liked a cup when you could get it.'

Victor was too surprised and pleased to speak, for a moment. Then he said, 'Go on, give us a kiss, darling.'

Mum laughed and waved him away. 'Hop off, you wicked old man. I'll have to watch you.'

Andrew looked at them both. They all knew that the coffee was probably terrible.

Before they reached Coltishall Andrew was afraid that today was going to be another dud. The sky was cloudy. There was nothing flying below the cloud and no sound from anything above it. They saw the yellow helicopter droning back to base but after it had gone the sky remained empty.

When they arrived at Firegate Four there were already several cars parked by the fence and people stood about with field glasses and radios.

'Crowds are gathering early,' said Victor, looking hopeful. 'Maybe they've got something big on.'

Over by the hangars the Lightnings stood in a line and figures moved among them.

'Something ought to happen soon,' said Andrew. 'They look pretty busy over there.'

'Which way's the wind blowing?' said Victor. 'I can see one moving now, but I think that's going the wrong way.'

Andrew looked at the windsock blowing fatly from its mast like the nipped-off finger of a rubber glove.

'Same way as before,' he said. 'I think that one's going into the hangar.'

It was, and a few moments later, another followed it.

'That's as bad as Monday,' said Victor, looking away. 'That's worse. Why get them out at all if they're only going to put them away again? Why don't they fly?' he asked himself aloud.

Andrew didn't try to answer but only cursed himself over their lost Thursday.

'Hold on,' said Victor. 'Something's on the move over there.'

A small tail fin could be seen, ziz-zagging in the distance. Then the plane to which it was attached, took off.

'Bloody Chipmunk!' roared Victor, slamming his hand down on top of the gate. A fang of barbed wire nicked the side of his finger and he swallowed anything else he might have said aand sucked it. One or two of the bystanders turned to look at him, unable to tell why he was so angry. They were delighted to see the Chipmunk. They were delighted to see anything, as long as it flew.

One family had brought along Granny and the baby, which seemed to have been a mistake. Father, who was eavesdropping on the control tower with a radio tuned to the aircraft frequency, suddenly announced, 'Apparently there is a plane going to overshoot the runway, coming now.'

Everyone looked towards the runway, expecting fire engines, drama and wreckage.

'That only mean that won't land,' said Victor to Andrew, and all that appeared was a small, twin-engined aircraft that went over, rather high up, and didn't come back.

'I suppose you could call that overshooting,' said Victor loudly. Father turned away and twiddled the controls officiously, zipping the aerial in and out, several times. Granny took the baby to look at the horses in the next field.

'Shall we go round to the end of the runway?' said Andrew, as he saw the scowl setting firm on Victor's forehead.

'Leave that a bit,' said Victor. 'Something's bound to happen soon.'

They waited and they waited. One of the cars drove away. Father, with the radio clapped to his ear said, 'There's a Spitfire taking off.'

'A likely story,' said Victor, under his breath.

But the Spitfire was taking off.

As it went by, Victor swarmed up the gate and waved madly. 'Scramble!'

In answer to his call a second Spitfire took off and soared above them. On the firegate Victor turned in giddy circles following their path over the trees. The first Spitfire began to climb but the second circled the field and skimmed low over the runway, upside down.

'That's the Victory Roll,' said Victor as the fighter righted itself and climbed again, veering to the left as it passed over them.

'If we'd come yesterday,' he said, 'we'd have missed all this. Here that come again. That's going to land. Oh, don't, don't,' he cried, in real pain at the thought that it might be over so soon.

165

The Spitfire climbed once more.

'I think he heard you,' said a voice at his elbow. Granny and the baby had come back from watching the horses. The baby hid its face and growled every time the Spitfire passed, but Granny, like Victor, was gazing up at the planes.

'My husband flew one of those,' she said. 'I used to stand in our garden and watch them come back. They weren't supposed to do Victory Rolls, but sometimes...'

Victor looked down at her, from the gate.

'Did he come back?' he asked.

Andrew had been wondering the same thing, but hadn't liked to ask.

'Usually,' said Granny. 'Once he baled out and once he ditched. He wasn't killed, if that's what you mean. He's at home now, cleaning out the gutter. The sparrows are nesting in it.'

Victor winced at the thought of a Spitfire pilot cleaning out his own gutter.

Another voice remarked that the first Spitfire was now at six thousand feet. It was the radio, yammering to itself on the bonnet of the car.

They looked up and saw the Spitfire, a dark cross, outlined against the clouds.

'There's a Lightning at the end of the runway now,' said Andrew.

'About time,' said Victor, leaning over the gate, to see. 'Whatever is that doing?'

Instead of positioning itself for take-off, the Lightning was turning round and round on the spot, like a fly that has fallen into the bath.

'Perhaps the pilot is having a fit,' said Andrew.

'I think he's waiting for something,' said Victor. 'See those dots?'

Above the end of the runway a row of dark dots was moving towards them. As they came closer, Andrew counted seven aircraft, strung out in a line. He could not identify them as any he had seen before.

'Oh,' said Victor. 'Oh, no. Jaguars.'

The seven Jaguars drew nearer, achingly slowly, and flew over the airfield, curving away behind the trees, still in the same, purposeful line.

'I don't think they're going to land,' said Andrew, craning his neck to watch them go. They were beautifully new and shiny, and slightly unreal, like the models in Victor's bedroom. Victor leaned back against the gate and watched the Spitfire, still cruising above him.

'They'll be back,' he said. 'They'll land. They wouldn't have come all this way for nothing.'

Behind them, the seven Jaguars made a wide, confident turn and swept back across the airfield. They were in no hurry. They turned again, making a last lap of honour before taking possession. Then the line broke and they spread out, one behind the other, for the final approach.

Victor was still watching the Spitfire.

'The Lightning's moving,' said Andrew. Victor looked over his shoulder.

'That won't take off now,' he said. 'That's going to lead them in.'

Above the shrilling of the Jaguars' engines they heard again the thunderous snarl of the Lightning. It passed slowly down the field and the first Jaguar landed in its wake, dropping elegantly onto the runway, its parachute snapping open behind. Perfectly distanced the other six followed it until they were all on the runway together, led by the Lightning.

The Jaguars were lean and beaky aircraft, their cockpits high off the ground, balanced above spindly legs. As each one rolled by Andrew caught a glimpse, underneath it, of the Lightnings, lined up with their backs to the newcomers. They looked heavy and clumsy and very, very old.

He glanced at Victor and saw that he, like the Lightnings, had turned his back on the Jaguars. He was looking down the lane.

'Everything go,' said Victor. 'Everything go that you like best. That never come back.'

'Let's go home,' said Andrew. 'There's nothing more to see. Shall we go?'

They took the bicycles from against the fence. Andrew stole a last look over his shoulder and saw another grey tailfin sliding furtively into the hangar.

When they reached the crossroads by the pub with the propeller on the wall, Victor said, 'We never had that coffee. I could do with that now.'

They leaned the bicycles against the hedge and Victor took the vacuum flask out of his saddle bag. He poured the coffee into the lid and offered it to Andrew.

'You first, it's supposed to be yours,' said Andrew.

Victor took a long and noisy swig and held out the lid again.

'Go on, finish it,' said Andrew. 'I'll have the next lot.'

'I'm not poisonous,' said Victor, but he took back the lid and drank down the coffee.

'This is the same as yesterday,' he said. 'Weren't you going to get instant coffee?'

'I meant to,' said Andrew, 'but I forgot. I went straight home again.'

'Did you, now,' said Victor, looking at him. 'Well I like this fine.' He tipped his head to get at the dregs and the coffee went up his nose, choking him. Andrew rescued the flask before he could jerk out the rest of the contents and Victor sat down on the grass to finish his seizure in comfort.

'What are you doing?' said Andrew. 'Trying to be a whale? You'll be blowing it out of your ears next.'

Victor laughed and blinked and sniffed. He drew the length of his sleeve across his face. Andrew couldn't see whether he was wiping his mouth, his nose or his eyes.

17 | What a Way to Go

Victor stayed away all weekend. Andrew took a couple of casual strolls past the end of the loke, once alone and once with Edward, hoping that the sight of the pram would lure Victor out. He saw no one but Victor's father, prowling through the dusk with his shotgun.

On Saturday night a gale blew up and tore down a branch from the oak tree at the end of the Skeltons' garden. When Andrew looked out of the landing window next morning he saw Victor's bedroom window peering beadily through the gap, and that night, when it grew dark, he saw the bomber's moon, glowing behind the curtains.

He pointed it out to Mum.

'Now you can signal to each other,' she said. 'You'd better learn Morse and I'll buy you an Aldiss lamp for Christmas.'

'I know some already,' said Andrew. 'I don't know if Victor could learn it though."

'He could if he wanted to,' said Mum. 'He might know it anyway. Don't jump to conclusions.'

'His writing looks like Morse,' said Andrew. 'All those full stops. I'll ask him when I see him. If I see him.'

'Why shouldn't you see him?' said Mum. 'He'll be around when he feels like it. Strange though it may seem, he'll get used to the idea of the Jaguars. You'll be going to Coltishall to see them instead. It's no good telling him that now, though. He wouldn't believe you.'

'I never thought he'd take it so bad,' said Andrew. 'I suppose he kept pretending it wouldn't happen. And it's only aeroplanes, after all.'

'What does he love better than aeroplanes?' said Mum. Andrew shrugged.

'Queen Kong, perhaps. I don't think so.'

'Well, he'll be round to see her even if he doesn't come to see you,' said Mum.

Andrew thought this was poor comfort. On Monday afternoon, when he opened the back door and saw Victor kneeling by the patent, monococque guinea-pig pen he remembered what she had said.

'Hello, said Andrew. 'Are you visiting us or the guinea-pigs?'

'I'm visiting you,' said Victor. 'But I had to say hello to Queenie first. I thought that if she got to know my footsteps she might whistle when she heard me coming.'

'Are you going to train her to fetch your slippers too?' asked Andrew, and then saw that Victor had been serious about wanting Queen Kong to whistle, when she heard his footsteps. He refrained from telling him that so far Queenie hadn't uttered a sound.

'Guinea-pigs aren't very clever,' he said. 'It might be a little while before she knows you.'

'I've brought your books back,' said Victor. 'And the thermos.'

'There was no hurry,' said Andrew, afraid that Victor was returning the things to save having to come round again.

'You might need them,' said Victor. 'Especially the thermos. I thought we might go to Marham tomorrow. That's where the Victors are. That's a long way.'

'Your namesakes,' said Andrew. 'Won't we have to take lunch? I'll ask Mum to make us something.'

'I hope she do,' said Victor. 'My Mum won't. She's not happy at the moment. A bit of our oak tree blew down on Saturday and went through the greenhouse. That didn't do the tomatoes any good.'

'I noticed,' said Andrew. 'I can see your bedroom window from our landing. I thought we could signal to each other. Could you learn the Morse Code?'

'I know that already,' said Victor. 'Don't look so surprised. My brother taught me that when he was home on leave. He rigged up a buzzer between his room and mine but my Dad tripped over the wire and fell downstairs. We had to take it away.'

'I know a little,' said Andrew. 'S.O.S. and I am listing to port, I got that out of a book. Could you teach me? Mum said she'd buy me an Aldiss lamp for Christmas. I'm not sure what that is. I think she was joking.'

'I reckon she was,' said Victor. 'That's one of those big signalling lamps. I know, when that get dark tonight I'll put the hundred watt bulb in and signal with the light switch. You see how much you understand. I'd better get back now. Dad's putting new glass in the greenhouse after tea. I've got to help him.'

Andrew saw Victor to the gate. As he was leaving he paused and held up his hand.

'Do you hear what I hear?'

'Lightning,' said Andrew. They both looked up.

From the direction of Coltishall came a single

Lightning. When it was immediately overhead it tilted and went into a vertical climb.

'Forty thousand feet in two and a half minutes,' whispered Victor.

It went up and up, hung for a second, then the nose came down and it fell in a long, solitary dive, until it levelled out and aimed itself homewards.

They watched it as long as it was visible above the horizon, and didn't speak until the thunder had died away.

'I wonder if that was the last Lightning of all,' said Andrew. It was a more splendid memory than the tamed and shabby tigers, slinking into the hangar and begging to be forgotten.

Victor grinned, his old and famous grin, and made a searing dive with his hand.

'Well, if that wasn't, that ought to have been. What a way to go out, eh? Whaaaaaaaam!'

Heard about the Puffin Club?

. . . it's a way of finding out more about Puffin
books and authors, of winning prizes (in
competitions), sharing jokes, a secret code, and
perhaps seeing your name in print! When you
join you get a copy of our magazine, *Puffin
Post*, sent to you four times a year, a badge
and a membership book.
For details of subscription and an application
form, send a stamped addressed envelope to:

The Puffin Club Dept A
Penguin Books Limited
Bath Road
Harmondsworth
Middlesex UB7 ODA

and if you live in Australia, please write to:

The Australian Puffin Club
Penguin Books Australia Limited
P.O. Box 257
Ringwood
Victoria 3134